Naranjo the Muse

a collection of stories

by

Omar S. Castañeda

Arte Público Press
Houston, Texas
1997

This volume is made possible through grants from the National Endowment for the Arts (a federal agency), the Andrew W. Mellon Foundation, The Cultural Arts Council of Houston and the Lila Wallace Reader's Digest Fund.

Recovering the past, creating the future

Arte Público Press
University of Houston
Houston, Texas 77204-2090

Cover illustration and design by Gladys Ramirez

Castañeda, Omar S., 1954-
    Naranjo the muse : a collection of stories /
by Omar Castañeda.
        p.   cm.
    ISBN 1-55885-192-5 (alk. paper)
    1. Fantastic fiction. American. I. Title.
PS3553.A8133N37   1997
813'.54—dc21   96-39821
                                                    CIP

The paper used in this publication meets the requirements of the American National Standard for Permanence of Paper for Printed Library Materials Z39.48-1984.♾

Naranjo the Muse

a collection of stories

Contents

I. Wounds

Misunderstanding Prufrock,
With Some Cummings 11
My Comrade Podvig 20
Love's Lost Labor: Male 32
Dogs of Clowerston 39
The Discovery Channel 75
The Rabbit War 77
God's Polyp 85
High on the Precipice 92

II. Into Pearls

The Song of Ishkik 99
The Grackle 105
Under a Blinding Sun 120
The Odd Time of Raúl Sombra 127
Office Games 135
Mything Linda in the High Window 143
The News of The Author 154
The English Professor 158

To my teachers Philip Appleman and Scott R. Sanders,
intellectual and moral guides far beyond their knowledge.

The following stories first appeared with modifications in:

Misunderstanding Prufrock, With Some cummings in
Currents from the Dancing River
My Comrade Podvig in *The Seattle Review*
Love's Lost Labor: Male in *The Kenyon Review*
Dogs of Clowerston in *The Americas Review*
The Discovery Channel in *Jeopardy*
The Rabbit War in *Jeopardy*
God's Polyp (as Cartographic) in *The Artful Dodge*
High on the Precipice in *River City Review*
The Song of Ishkik in *The Raven Chronicles*
The Grackle in *Calapooya Collage*
Under a Blinding Sun in *Special Report: Fiction*
The Odd Time of Raúl Sombra in *Pencil Press Quarterly*
Office Games in *River City Review*

"Of course, through deceit and self-deceit, we cloistered writers hope our wounds will be turned into pearls."
— *Cassandra Mateo*

I. WOUNDS

Misunderstanding Prufrock,
With Some Cummings

Long before Dian sleeps with him, she knows, she is certain of it!—all there is to know of him.

She kept him for weeks just under her tongue, his heat cupped in her palms, his softness behind her knees. She thought everyone could smell his scent on her. It trailed her to his class, perfumed out when she crossed her long, long—Oh God, so long—legs. (White stockings suddenly looming brightly on the expanse of her thigh—like the sea foaming up, crashing, perhaps; the concussion of wild nature loud in the heart, loud in the empty chambers of our body. We could tell you—listen: Where she walked, moons and Saturn rings, vast nebulae, whole clusters of galaxies sprinkled down like argentum, that we faithfully mined. But this is another story. A story that breaks our heart.)

Dr. Naranjo saw none of this. For Dian, the scent of him followed her everywhere down the hallways, to the bathrooms in Ballantine Hall, where she scrubbed and scrubbed to remove her shame.

"My life is a nightmare of predictability," she told us.

She thought she might become a terrier, her toenails clicking in his kitchen, her head cocked expectantly at his door, her tongue flicking up. Once, sillily, she thought she would circle his mountain goat rug—of course, he would have one, a deep shag white, we were sure!—until curling comfortably at his feet.

She would accept a woman wanting him in front of the fire—their drinking of blood-red wines, their laughter, the woman's smooth delicious throat. She would content herself with his fingers under her muzzle, scratching, his large hand stroking the arch of her back. All because someday he would make room for her on his bed, say in his husky, sonorous voice, "That's my good girl," or "Yeah-ess: Princess, Bay-bee, Sweet-ums." And there in his sheets, she would ascend into metamorphic dreams.

On Tuesdays, with the regularity of ash, she waited in the alcove beside his office, her back to the hall. Despite herself, she always imagined him coming out of his room, asking her for a piece of paper to write a quick note for another student. "Oh," she'd hear him say, "you got, maybe, a piece of scrap paper or something," his eyes not really looking, not really stopping, but scurrying over the flat surfaces of the alcove.

In this dream, she pulls out a Bic pen, blue, and places the thin blade in her hands. The ink bleeds through her skin and is siphoned up by his fingertips. She is perspiring, nibbling her inner lip, until she can't take it anymore, and flees. "Hey!" he shouts. "I just wanted a goddamned scrap from you." His voice is very high; his forearms are veined with ink, his mouth dribbles blue. "Just something! Just a little bit of nothing!" But his voice is so far away, trailing, diminishing, like a tail of comet dust so that all of this dream is indecipherable, intractable.

On Wednesdays, she watched him from a campus park bench and found something of a dromedary in him: his long neck and reflective pose; his woolly chin-chin.

On Thursdays, she cracked pistachios between her knees and waited for him to appear and for her breath to disappear. Always, it was the secretive dip of his fingers into his inner coat pocket that sent her writhing, salty red spots dappling her knees.

On weekends, she imagined two-hundred phone calls.

Courting? This?

When she finally sleeps with him—did we mention the heavens raining from her like angel dust?—it is *his* back that grows curly black hair. Yes. *He* growls into her ear. His face lengthens. His nose grows cold. He laps affectionately at her throat. He, ha-ha, he!

"Sit!" she says. "Heel!" She falls impatiently back into his pillow and lights a Camel Filter.

He whimpers away.

Blue smoke rises to the ceiling. She can hear him lapping his red thing, and wonders how she ever thought he was so?

He crouches in the corner.

Handsome? Dangerous?

One of his legs paddle-wheels at a flea, and scratches against the blue shag rug.

"God, Naranjo. It's not like we promised each other any-thing."

"Yip."

"I was honest with you from the start."

"Woof."

Another whorl of smoke, blue above her. Her hand droops to the edge of the bed. She feels exhausted. The affair is already... "God. Okay," she says.

He comes trailing an ecstatic spray of pee. Yellow.

"I'm sorry," she says.

His tail slices the air.

There is power yet in those beagle eyes. Her heart unfrowns. "Was it anything I did?"

"No," he whispers, feeling the bones of his teeth shrink back. "No."

She is distracted. "Sure?"

"It was me."

"Hmm?" She watches his ears shorten; lobes begin to appear.

"I mean it was me."

"M-hmm?" She remembers the smell of a Baskin-Robbins, long ago. When? Where? One where we were whiling away time.

"I mean, why—that is when—I asked for, you know, you to lie down..."

She smiles distractedly. "Yes-ums?"

"Down, lie down," he said. "With the begonia over your ear. And the butter dribbled... "

"Better?"

"Butter. Are you deaf?"

"But you wanted it *melted*."

The word alone brings back his erection.

She giggles. "It was too hot."

His tongue flicks up against her earlobe.

"You're my professor!" she whines affectedly. Her long fingers curl lightly around him.

Naranjo shudders. He leans his head back to better feel her intimate caress. Ah, but something else takes hold of him and he suddenly crumples into her lap.

"What?" she asks.

He squirms.

"What?"

His fur reappears. His paws grow hard curved nails.

"I'm afraid," he confesses.

Dian nods. "Me too." And softer, her voice bruised, her voice filling with something genuine, something that stings us: "Me too, Naranjo."

Because of this, a man stands humiliated atop a building and looks down on the trees facing this literature professor's colonial house. "Aargh!" we hear. Or perhaps, "It's me! Why can't you see this?" Or, "Oh! Oh! Oh!"—It is a voice. Atop a brown building. That much is certain.

"What am I going to do?" she asks us.

Our throat is sore, hoarse. "Do you love him?" Already feeling the words galloping away.

"He wants everything so secret."

Our napkin is twisted into a grotesque ice-cream cone.

"I *was* his student."

"Is he... is he the most important thing to you?"

She looks over her shoulder. "Not now, though."

"Not now?"

Turning back: "Are you deaf? I'm not in his class anymore."

We do not like the small explosion of impatience in her throat.

"It's not like he's married or anything." The salt and pepper shakers collide in her hands.

"Perhaps you're just infatuated with him."

She rubs the holes of the silver shakers together. "We get along pretty well."

"Just a passing thing, perhaps. Meaningless."

"Odd how we can talk. You know, really talk."

"An infatuation of the body," we venture.

Her eyes glance at the door.

We venture again: "I always assumed that you and... "

"There are some moments with him that... "

"And us? What about us?"

"...are incredibly enlightening."

She did not hear. "Like lighting a kerosene-soaked cat!?"

The salt shakers are suspended in air. "I beg your pardon?"

We pull the shakers from her hands. "I think you do this too often."

"What are you talking about?" she says.

"This thing with authority figures."

"Oh, give me a... "

"No! You get all wrapped up in a professor and you think it's love or something."

"That's not... "

"It's a little embarrassing to see you do this." We look around the room for ears and eyes. "Do you think you may have a little problem here? I mean with really connecting, maybe? Being whole?"

"That's not... "

"What is it with you, anyway, that makes you have to be in a position of subservience? Of looking up to men? Why do you have to do this? It's humiliating. I mean... "

She is on her feet. "That is not it at all!"

"Then what is it?"

"Not at all!" she growls.

A veritable bang of asteroids, photinos, quasars and red-shifts follow her out. We are certain she will go to him.

We see her next at three in the morning, saying she fell asleep in the Clowerston Library (it closes at nine). She spends an eternity with her tortoise-shell comb before going to sleep. We watch her in the mirror: eyes closed; arms undulating and entwining like broad sea plants; her face a blush of red; her breathing under a lunar spell; her hips grinding, grinding the soft white ottoman. Her nakedness becomes an exquisite tragedy of curves and shadows, a deep-set bowl of hips, thighs, abdomen, and—within this pale chalice—her dark-haired pudendum.

We cannot get angry. We cannot even speak. She is too?

Suddenly we envision an impossibility: her body menstruating, filling that Grail of her hips and thighs with life-rich blood, and we on our knees before her, soul aching for redemption, tongue for mass.—

Ethereal? Divine?

"I think we should end this," she says. Her eyes are on us.

We can barely swallow. We swipe a forearm across our vision-stained lips.

"'Our now must come to then,'" she quotes from cummings.

Her knees uncross, the bowl falls apart.

"'Our then shall be some darkness.'"

"Can't I please stay forever in your pockets?"

"No."

"Just take me out when you want to, when you want to..."

"Really, no."

"It doesn't matter. I can wait; I can be there for you. Keep me in a drawer. That's all I ask."

She is pulling away.

"Under some sweaters, or old bras." We are driving her away. "It doesn't matter! I can wait. I'll stay out of your way, until you want me again."

"Look... "

"I can be alone until you're ready. Please. I won't even think of it as suffering."

"That's not... "

Suddenly, we are on our feet and screaming at the top of our lungs, "What do you want me to do!"

In an instant, finality molds her face.

"I'm sorry," she states flatly. Her hands gather air toward her. "I'm really sorry, Alfred. Really."

But this is the other story.

Dian leaves us in the morning, bookbag clutched tight at her side. She will see him. Him. Him. At the head of the class, speaking out, book clutched tight in his mitt, correcting sophomoric understandings of Modernism, of "Prufrock," of mermaids singing. "'I should have been a pair of claws scuttling across the floor of the sea,'" he says. She swooning at such unbridled passion, such denial of effete intellectualism. We mumbling, "You're damn right, asshole."

Here is the real story.

They meet furtively under the maples that shield his car. Drive away, her head held down as they pass campus security. Her laughter bubbles up at their escapade. Her hands open the knot of hair at her nape; she shakes free great cascades of deep galactic black. She watches for his street. His house, with large scented bathtub, wide marble kitchen counters, four-poster bed with four loose nooses, high-armed chairs for looping legs, pillows mushrooming on floors, large hanging baskets, oils, lotions, circular seats with holes, vibrating things, long tickling ostrich things, feathers and boas, fuming incense, mist sprays, and silky, lavish protuberances.

Later, she wants to go to a movie. Or rent. "I don't know, something with Cary Grant, maybe."

He has to prepare for classes. There's a meeting. "Not this time, okay?"

She growls affectionately, barks, and they crash into each other again. And so it goes, in this minuscule story. Until finally, through the spray, she sees him for what he is.

We imagine them walking together on campus, pretending a seemly relationship. Deferential. Underneath, something quite different. Something boiling up. Something tied to his conspiratorial wave to a male colleague and his light-hearted scampering ahead.

"You're the most selfish man I've ever known!" she yells.

He turns on the steps of Ballantine Hall and glares back at her. Other students stop and stare. A window opens above them.

"All you want is someone who adores you! Someone who thinks you're special! What have you given me in return? Huh?"

Another window screeches open, old paint relenting. Then quickly, so that Dian backs away in momentary fear, he rushes headlong toward her, like a truck, a red and yellow pickup truck.

"Okay," he says. "Let's try this. I'm sorry. I see how I have done wrong. I have not given you enough power in this. I see how I have misunderstood."

Her mouth twists.

"But I can do better. I can. I know I've acted badly. Please. We can try. I can try. If you let me. That is." He pats his human legs as proof of sincerity.

She, of course, is a barnacle to hope. "Okay," she whispers. "Okay." She feels too many eyes upon them.

He spreads his arms to embrace the entire campus. His voice rises far above a whisper, far above propriety, and into a clear blue decision. "Let's go camping this weekend! Tomorrow, I mean. Right now, I mean!"

She laughs at his exuberance.

"I'm dead serious!"

"Oh, Naranjo."

"Just you and me," he whispers.

Already his hands are warming her shoulders.

"Tomorrow's fine," she answers, pouting shyly, forgiving him with upturned mouth, forgiving herself her submission.

But he will not kiss her unless she is absolutely certain that this is her decision, too. "I really do love you, you know?"

Her eyelids drop. Her shoulders slacken. Her knees grow hair.

He brings her mouth to his.

It isn't until their seventh day that she decides to shave his beard. Razor in hand, strop at the ready, the Coleman lamp casting rooster shadows, she approaches the cot. Far above the tent, a pair of bats jag through the night, the horned moon lows through grazing clouds. Frogs bark and pop.

The professor is dead drunk. He is spent.

She, in our story, has had enough of panfish, of small white scales, of campfires. Of getting. She has had enough of scrubbing the scent of fish from her body. She has had it with the minnows that swim through her pores when he falls on top of her. She wants a trimming.

So, in this story, when she finishes with his hairy face, it is as if she has cut off his.

Clippings fall onto a bag of Dick Loeb's Unsalted Peanuts.

Nose? Thumbs? Feet?

Hah! we hear. Hah! Atop a brown building.

My Comrade Podvig

Raoul stroked the animal's rump as if in a daze. The bristles whisked back and forth, back and forth until we were sure the beast would flare against him. His boyish face was as ruddy as the horse's coat.

We decided to throw pebbles at him, one at a time and increasing the size of the missiles until he stirred from his daydreaming. We wagered on how long it would take. Alexus, who called him Podvig* because of his abstruseness, wanted to throw sticks, but we all agreed that would be too much. I started with a jagged stone that clacked on the ground beside him. The second throw still didn't rouse him. We continued the game, mocking his obliviousness, and paused only once as the guard captain passed along the rampart. Finally, a misplaced shot hit Raoul firmly on the leg. He jumped to attention while saluting the horse and the air. We roared with laughter; he turned slowly toward us, his hand remaining up to his brow even as he realized the ploy.

*["podvig" in Russian means holy exploit, an acetic journey.]

I stepped away from the others and walked to him, laughing kindly now and hoping he would take it all as gentle teasing rather than as heartless ridicule.

"Raoul," I called out, "come on now. Smile!"

The corners of his eyes tightened.

"Listen. Come on, Raoul." I touched him and pulled him closer. "I have a secret for you. Listen." I put my arm over his shoulder so that I could whisper by his ear. "You know that the only sin is despondency? Of course you do! You know the story. Come on. The tale of the two hermits. Told by Varsonophy: 'There are no sins of any importance save despondency.' Remember? You know it well, don't you? Of course! Make your name ring, Raoul!" I slapped his back. "From Alexandria to Byzantium, Kiev to Moscow! Ah, Raoul."

He smiled weakly.

The others waited, hoping, I guessed, for some new kind of jest. When it became apparent that the play had ended, Alexus called out for all to go for drinks. Raoul shrank away.

"When are you free?" I asked.

"Soon," he said, his head hanging low.

Alexus slapped at the air in our direction, as if he were shooing away gnats, then led the others toward the inn. Raucous laughter broke from them as they turned from sight.

"Who takes over?" I asked, turning him by the elbow and keeping an eye out for the guard captain.

"Vladimir."

"I'll wait. We'll go to the inn together."

"There's no need," he said.

Raoul stared sadly at the ground. "Of course there isn't." I wanted his spirits to lift. "I'll wait." It would be good to talk a bit over drinks.

"Thank you, but I must finish the rounds before Vladimir arrives. I cannot stand here any longer."

"Yes, of course." I lifted my hand and waved him off with the tips of my fingers, feeling instantly presumptuous for doing so. It was a gesture of St. Petersburg dandies. Raoul, however, took the kindly motion for what it was and turned to his duty. He disappeared around the smithy.

I did not wait long before Vladimir came staggering from behind the corral. He rubbed his unshaven chin with his knuckles so vigorously that I wondered whether it was his hand or his chin that itched.

"Ugh," he said. "What a party, Vizhnik."

The stink of stale alcohol and cigarettes crinkled my nose.

"Too much drinking...." He put a hand to his head and moaned. "Moderation," he said.

The small wave of visitors to the fort parted around a gentleman who had halted to stare at us across the open field. He wore one brown shoe and one black shoe.

"One must know moderation in this world," Vladimir continued. "Moderation and tolerance! There are no higher virtues."

"Except duty," I added, keeping him at arm's length.

He groaned. "Yes, yes, except duty."

"You're here for the guard?"

"I've come to relieve our Raoul—our Podvig, as Alexus says." He looked around. "Where is our beacon?"

Before I could answer, Vladimir stood at ragged attention and gestured broadly: "Where is our Podvig?" he said with great intonation, then confided in me, "Do you know that he's gone into caring for the mortar of the walls of our fortress? What a man! The mortar! He cares, Vizhnik, he cares. I'll wager he's sitting at this very moment watching insects battling and evolving by the walkways. He cares, Vizhnik." Vladimir laughed briefly, then put his hand to his brow. "Oh, my head!"

"Moderation, my dear Vladimir."

"Ugh!" He grimaced valiantly against his hangover. "Alexus and the others—did they go to the inn?"

"Yes."

"Well, comrade, onward, onward!" He thrust his arm into the air. "Duty first, then pleasure. I beg your pardon: Duty *is*

pleasure." He sheathed his saber hand in his shirt front and
left to find Raoul.

"Tell him that I'm waiting for him," I said.

"Waiting for Podvig?" he asked with amusement.

I grimaced at his pun. "I want to talk with him."

"Of course," he said, chuckling.

He vanished yet returned shortly, speaking loudly of moderation with an arm draped over Raoul's shoulder, his chest
swollen oratorically. Vladimir paused while he lectured to pick
lint from Raoul's uniform.

Vladimir gave Raoul a final tidying over and terse admon-
ishment, then sent him off with a sharp slap on the back.
Raoul hurried toward me, his eyes spilling over with enthusiasm.

"He's right," Raoul said. "Vladimir is right, Vizhnik. Moderation is the way!"

He stopped abruptly, searched in his pockets, but found
nothing.

"But moderation can't help when we change. Can I only
moderately move? Can I only moderately take my belongings
and go to the Solovyof? No! I must take it all or not at all."

Raoul turned, stamped his foot decisively and turned
again.

"Yes!"

I was, admittedly, bewildered. "What on earth are you
talking about?"

"I must move, Vizhnik."

"What? Where?" His whole body seemed a gangly mad-
ness.

"There's a house by the Solovyof. I've asked the Comman-
dant. He'll let me know."

"But why? What are you talking about?"

"To change!" He waved his arms over his head.

"What? Change what?"

He ignored me, and peered over my shoulder to spy surreptitiously.

"Change what?" I repeated, looking behind me. There was nothing.

His face reddened. He slapped his chest vigorously, as if striking a deep drum, then whispered so softly I could barely hear him. "To change... To change..."

I thought a lack of food might be the cause of his anxiety. "Let's eat," I suggested, and tried to take his arm. "The inn's ambrosia."

He pulled away. "No," he said softly. He tilted his head and listened. He stood on his toes and peered behind me again.

I turned again and again saw nothing.

"When was the last time you ate? Come on, Raoul. We're friends. Let's go to the inn and we'll eat."

"No. I don't want to eat. I want to go outside the camp."

"We'll drink vodka and coffee. You can tell me about the house." It was perfectly obvious that he heard nothing from me.

"There's a hill just outside," he said. "If we go now, right now, it's very close. Come with me."

I let him see my disbelief.

"Please," he said, for once truly looking into my eyes. "You must come with me. I want to speak to you. There's something very important."

Before I could respond, he stepped away and walked to the gate, as if there was no question but that I would do as he asked.

"Come quick!" he shouted, without looking back. "You've never seen this."

"Wait!" It seemed as if the very word sprang from my throat and attached to him like a gaff, but instead of it pulling him back, he pulled me forward.

"Come," he said.

I followed.

"Faster!" he called.

I ran as hard as I could, but the distance between us slowly increased. Part of my surprise, I guess now—much later, staring up into the cobwebbed vault of my barracks and again reliving that vague time when I heard voices, human voices, and drowned, too—was that I followed this madman. His shout pulled me forward as we ran and it took several minutes before I realized that it was the name of Antero Vipunen that he called out like some battle cry. Why would he call that wizened man's name?

He rushed a steep hill, then passed from sight just above the crest. When I finally reached the peak, I was panting so hard that I leaned over, hands to my knees. Raoul sat cross-legged, staring out over the valley.

He slowly stretched his arm out, pointing. "Look," he said. "Do you see the world?"

I nodded, still trying to catch my breath.

"I knew you could!" he said. "They named you well, Vizhnik."

He closed his eyes and pointed toward me. A difference of air suddenly slipped over him like a cloak. He no longer seemed the same man, the same Podvig, the man who saved chicken bones and birds' wings.

"What is it?" I whispered, a little afraid.

"Sit down, friend." His voice had changed as well. It deepened in tone, became fuller, sonorous. "I want you to watch over me. You'll see very soon. Sit."

I obeyed him, folding my legs beneath me as best I could. He reached out to clasp my hand tightly, painfully. He faced the sun and intoned his words religiously.

"We shall roll upwards, Vizhnik. Yes, immaculately rolling up. I can hear the world's wheels whirring on. 'Come,' they say. 'Come, come on; come, come on. Onward.' "

I was dumfounded. The difference in Raoul's presence came as a lightness within me, not so much as something suddenly enveloping him. It nearly took my breath again, so that I deliberately closed and reopened my eyes to remove the spell upon us. But I was not imagining it. Still, there was no physical difference in Raoul—it was something inside, something within me, somewhere behind my eyes, my mind, the bones of my skull. Even now it is hard to explain. It is impossible! His fingers twitched and his feet tapped quietly the dirt. That is all I can explain.

The instant I noticed his limbs, I saw the image of the shaman, Vipunen—but where the image was, I cannot say. It was real, that much I know. And there was a definite knocking across my brow. I understood that Raoul had slipped away and was now, like some celestial worm, knocking at the gate of my brow. And there, in that strange, arcane moment, it seemed no difficult thing for him to enter.

I was wrong, however. It was not as a worm or snake that he burrowed into my thoughts, but as the famous sage, Vainamoinen. I saw him standing by a vast expanse as he worked on a barge. Everything was perfectly clear: The vessel had splintered under the poet, broken from under the singer. Vainamoinen had made a boat of Knowledge, but he lacked three words to fix it. The sage slowly looked at me, in those liquid swells of dreams, and told me to watch while he left for an auger from *Podvizhnitchestvo*. I would know how long to wait, he said. Then I was to call him back to Raoul's body. If I waited too long, the body would rot, be impossible to return to such a fetid form. I must not forget, I was told, nor take too long in this watch over Podvig. "Do not fail!" the voices said.

Then, with a somber, gray-haired nod, the singer left for the tool to finish his boat. There, at the river to *Ecstasy*, as it is sometimes called, the daughter of *Death* chided him.

"What brought you here?" she asked.

The poet did not mince his words. "Fire brought me here. Fire, that wonderful wizard."

"If fire had brought you here," she said, "your clothes would be burned. They would carry the odor of char, my friend."

Vainamoinen replied quickly, unruffled: "By water. I came as we usually travel. I came by water."

The guardian merely laughed. She crouched and clutched her stomach in fits of laughter. She touched his dry clothes.

Next, the sage said that he had come by iron.

"Now I know you are a liar!" she shouted. "If death had brought you here, your face would carry gore. Now, the truth!"

"I'll tell the truth," he said. "I came looking for the gimlet to fix my barge. The Old Shaman, Highest One, has the words."

The daughter of the gate smiled victoriously. "It's a most ferocious fool who comes this way. Come in, come in."

At that moment, a shrill whistle from the camp told me that my turn for duties was near. I wanted to stay and watch, but the call was made. Would I have to choose between these two? What choice did I have? What choice do I have? The whistle, Siren of peculiar desires, came again.

The guardian brought a raft for Vainamoinen to cross. It came with a third whistle, so that I drifted from the scene. The whistle had come from without. Within, they rowed across the narrows, where the poet would be given a bed for rest.

The covers would have to keep watch! I left Raoul where he sat. He didn't move, but sat staring out over the valley. I urged him to come, but he sat like an apple—oblivious to me.

As I walked back to the camp, as I waited and prepared for my duties, as I completed my rounds, as I flicked the hairs from my uniform, I kept an eye out for Raoul. He was not required to return until well into nightfall, but it was unheard of for Raoul to miss his coffee and vodka.

Much later, still disturbed by Raoul's absence, I brushed the Captain's mare and watched.

Alexus entered the hooped light of the barn.

"Still looking?" he asked.

"It's strange for him to miss his meal. Something has happened." How could I explain to Alexus what I had seen? Perhaps I was to blame.

"Maybe he finally got tired of doing all these stupid rounds and combing of horses and guarding. What's it for, anyway?"

"That's you?" I asked. "I don't believe it."

"Well, yes! Even I get tired of all this, Vizhnik. Even I."

"You're drunk."

"A little."

I patted the Captain's horse. "Can you imagine Raoul tired of all this?"

We both looked around the barn as if taking the question literally. It was a silly question. The days of our lives were counted by duties and incessant rounds that earned us our room and board and the slow accumulation of extra comforts, but not one of us had any idea as to why the fort was where it was, or who brought the orders to our captain on the ramparts. We had long ago given up the question as to our ultimate commander. We obeyed the bugles and whistles. We obeyed the duty rosters, the calls to inspection. We passed each other, saluted, handed down the orders of the day and found ways to forget our stations when we were free of duties. Who could understand any of it? These were the ideas of our lives. We had what was sufficient, we knew what was sufficient: *That* was our Commander—Sufficiency.

I brushed the horse vigorously. "He's a fool!"

Alexus steadied the horse's head. "Those eyes, Vizhnik, have been looking where you and I can't imagine. I'm sure of it." The mare shook free her head, the long mane flipping wildly. "Who knows what's in his mind? He's a visionary, perhaps. Our Podvig! No, visionaries are much too tied to the world. Even more than we are. Since they constantly search for ways to transcend the earth, they must constantly think of the earth. We, on the other hand, are carefree. We have our boots to the earth and no sky crosses our eyes. And we can drink the earth right out of our heads whenever we wish. We are the freest!"

I grunted. "We do what we must, I guess."

"It doesn't matter, anyway," he said, slapping the dust free of his pants. "It's my turn by the Relic tonight."

"Yes?" It meant that I would be guarding it soon. Sooner than I had thought.

"Duty!" he said. "We'll see each other, comrade. Don't waste time on Raoul." He flourished his arm. "To the Relic!"

I nodded, watching him walk away and out of the extension of lamplight by the door. A small cloud of dust swept back from his formal marching: his feet stamping flat the packed earth beneath us. I sensed the Relic in the musty smell kicked up.

By midnight, I had mulled over the goings-on of Raoul so many times that I was utterly confused. Duty called again in the morning. There is no bigger crime than to forsake one's duty. I tried to sleep, and gradually felt foolish for thinking that Raoul held such importance. I laughed at myself for worrying to such extremes. Still, the three words were tools that seemed at the very center of Raoul's journey—hallucination, my hallucination? But I had seen him entranced! I had seen him become Vipunen and then Vainamoinen. I had witnessed the search for the three words as clearly as I saw, and see *now*, the captain's mare, the ramparts, the perpetuity of the fortress.

But I had seen it all inside my head.

It was a puzzle of threes. Three words, three sages, three times the questions. I had seen something I cannot explain. Something for which language is inadequate.

I couldn't sleep. I had to find Raoul, if for no other reason than to protect myself from his apparent desertion. Alexus wouldn't help me look. Vladimir might be intrigued enough to search, but few of the men would carry on for very long without concrete rewards. A search for Podvig was a search too difficult, and by mid-journey a long and lonely search. No one would join me. Some of them laughed.

Then the question of whether or not to take the trip by myself became the difficult one. The whole affair seemed, by the others' lack of interest, to be even more of a foolish illusion. It felt as if I were about to take a phenomenally long voyage. The weight of it was at the same time exhilarating and oppressive. I recalled the lines of the Prague writer concerning a similar trek: "No provisions can save me. For it is, fortunately, a truly immense journey." Therein lay courage.

And leaving is finally easier than continuing.

Remembering the hill to be just outside the camp, I traveled in the dark without the aid of a torch. I traveled and traveled, well into the night, surprised at how far it had become. I repeated to myself that it was near. It was near. It was near.

First, I went by way of men's swords, my feet falling on the weapons' edges. Next, I turned to follow a way on the points of women's needles. There was no sign of Raoul. Then, by chance, I smelled the pungent earth alongside a hill and tracked it upward.

But the mound had grown in the night. A great ash tree stood tall on the shoulder of the knoll. An alder had grown from the jaw of the mound, and a bird-cherry rooted itself within the hill's beard. There was no mistake here: This was not the crest I had previously climbed with Raoul, but the huge and rotten head of Antero Vipunen. The sunken eyes whirred like windy caves, bat-filled and dank. The ears were stony crags. And from the gaping, root-choked maw came Raoul's voice.

"Come, come on," it chanted. "Come, come on."

I understood, then, the danger of all journeys: It is never easy to continue, never certain, never real. Every journey an allegory! Everything of the world fights these searches. Everything screams of material. Everything urges us toward nothing, urges us to live in life the antithesis of life, to squander what true spirit there may be on the torpid and the material and the utterly senseless. And to shun the crystalline air constantly surrounding us.

So then, with my flesh crawling, my stomach roaring, a wonder trembling through my sapling hands, I pleaded: "Podvig, Podvig!" hoping to hear that beautiful human voice, hear it not as human, but as a sylvan chime, one that could lure me on through the coldest channels of the earth and bring me to a great light.

Ah, Podvig. In the ceilings and floors and walls, I imagine these patterns still. Like faint maps of strange countries.

Love's Lost Hunger: Male

I. Pillow Talk

It started with you buried up to your neck in sand by the sea. There's an African boy standing beside you with a club you've given him. He's swinging it like a golf club, but it isn't an ordinary golf club. It has a razor edge that will sever your neck. The flat face will send your head into the sea. See, you want him to do it. You asked him to do it. You're calm. In some way, this is penitence. But each time the boy swings, you yell "Eyes! Eyes!" because the boy keeps missing and knocking sand into your face. He doesn't understand English, but he knows what you mean since your face is so expressive. The boy's family and friends watch from red and white tents, but they get bored. Some of them leave. The boy keeps trying. One time, he has to whisk away sand from the pocket of your mouth.

Behind him, there's a small parade of Africans nearing us. At first it looks like oil spreading over the sand. You see them, too, and get angry. The newcomers are carrying a lion. You shout at them and the lion turns its head. I see the strong and youthful face and think that it is smiling. I'm really very frightened until you tell me that lions can't smile.

At first you're angry with them. You tell me that they're going to dismember the lion. They'll strip off the skin and eat the meat from the lion's head. You ask me if I remember your restaurant in Texas where you served meat not only from the lion's head, but from its entire body. Your voice is so soft, so urgent. You desperately want me to remember your achievement. "I didn't waste anything!" you shout at them. Even then, you confide sadly to me, you hated Africans for leaving the limbs of lions scattered on beaches.

For some reason, I was living proof that your restaurant was decent and legitimate. And yet, I have done something that destroyed your good image. Most people have forgotten you, but because of what I have done you are buried neck deep in the sand. I want the people in the tents to know the truth about you, those people in parade to know. That's why I did something terrible.

The boy swings again and misses. Suddenly, I realize that I have been dreaming all along: We aren't facing the sea; we have been looking landward, staring at the infinite sand. The slight rolls of windswept desert fooled me into thinking of the sea. Or maybe I wanted the sea as much as you wanted me to remember... What? When I turn to look at the water, I know that the arid sand and the virile sea are equally beautiful.

I walk out over the rolling dunes and into the desert. I try to remember what it was that I had said or done to get you buried alive, but nothing comes. I expect to hear your death scream coming from over the dunes. Like the waste of lion's meat, it all seems so inevitable. But under the heat of the sun, you just melt away. Everything—the tents, the Africans, the dismembered lion with its haunting grin—everything melts into the vast and empty desert. I melt away, too, in that perfect emptiness. Not even a footprint of our passing.

II. Missives

Alfred coughed next to Dian. Her eyelids were still. He sat beside her head and touched her shoulder. The shoulder felt warm and pliable. He stood and said her name in a normal voice. He asked if she would be working late again. She made no reply. He told her he got a raise at work. Twice his salary. She did not move. He then slid the closet door open and lowered the blue suitcase. Now there were two letters underneath. He took the new letter into the bathroom.

His face flushed as he read the letter and, when he was finished, he unzipped his pants and urinated. He urinated against the basin to avoid the sound of splashing. Then he leaned over the sink and stared into his own eyes.

Kato barked.

Quickly, he put the letter and suitcase back. He stood over Dian again. Her mouth was partly open, the pillow damp from breathing. Alfred opened her underwear drawer and rummaged through these clothes she never wore. He made sure the articles remained as they had been before he touched them. He opened another drawer and searched. Alfred searched through all five of her drawers, but still did not find what he wanted.

He leaned breathlessly over the chest and bowed his head. Directly in front of him, Dian's jewelry box held what he had looked for. He lifted the small tape measure key chain from among the necklaces and ankle bracelets and read the words "Fran's Goodyear" written in red letters on the radial-tire look-alike. Slowly, he pulled the tape inch by inch until he saw the bright red heart drawn with magic marker. His scrotum shriveled. He licked his finger and ran it down the concave tape. The groove was just wide enough to accommodate the very tip of his finger. A red shadow smeared a quarter of an inch from the drawn heart. Alfred stared into his eyes in the mirror above the dresser, then he dropped the tape measure back into Dian's jewelry box.

Downstairs, Alfred did push-ups until his arms would not hold his weight. He turned over and lifted his legs a foot above the floor. When his muscles began to clench, he brought his hands from behind his head and pounded his stomach, beating it until it hurt. He alternated between push-ups and leg-lifts for nearly an hour, the adrenaline running like fire inside him. As he drank from the water pitcher in the refrigerator, his arms shook uncontrollably.

With that, he felt his penis stirring. He bounded up the stairs and undressed. He touched himself to erection as he crawled next to Dian. She shrugged when he opened her legs. She was wet. He entered her. Dian opened her eyes and groaned. "No, Babe," she said. Alfred moved slowly inside her. She placed her hand against his neck and spoke quietly. "Please, Alfred, I'm too tired." He quickened his movements. Dian sighed loudly and opened her legs to give him more freedom. She let her head fall sleepily to one side. Alfred pushed feverishly inside her for a minute or two, then tightened in orgasm. Dian smiled up with her eyes closed. "That was nice," she said, her eyes still closed, her head lolling. "That was nice."

Alfred slowed his breathing, feeling the pulse rack at his temples, and watched Dian fall back asleep. Exhausted, he drifted off by concentrating on the black inside his eyelids.

III. Dégringolade

On the return, Leticia again leans over your lap and once more her rounded mouth blows hot circles into your thigh.

By that evening, everyone who entered the bar knows about your trip to the river. What they know you do not know.

They say that Leticia's mother has punished her. They say you must excuse yourself to her.

When you go the next morning, Leticia is nowhere in sight. Her mother smiles nicely and invites you to wait in the house. You can see her outside through gaps in the branch wall as she dips water from an oil drum. She scrubs her hands well, then throws the water to the ground. Inside, coffee perks on a metal sheet over a concrete firestove. Smoke curls up through the flue in the ceiling.

Leticia's mother enters and asks you to sit at the table. A chicken, tied to a table leg, pecks the ground in a vain search for food. You sit away from the chicken. Leticia's mother pulls up a box to sit directly in front of you. Your gender is privilege. You beg for her forgiveness. You plead ignorance of the customs.

"I asked her if they intended anything," she says. "She said no and, of course, I have to believe her."

"Yes," you say.

"What worries a mother is that a daughter may get a bad reputation. She knows she cannot ride unaccompanied with men. She said that they didn't have bad intentions."

"Oh, no," you say.

"It's the people without culture who look down on that sort of thing. I'm sure in the capital women walk where they please. In the United States women don't ask permission to go. It's culture. And here there is no culture. The people here don't understand. People see her go and right away they think the men have ruined her."

"Oh, no," you say.

"It's the customs here," she continues. "Here a couple never touches. They don't hold hands. God forbid if they should touch. And a kiss—oh, no! A kiss and it's all over."

"Means marriage," you say.

"My God! The people don't understand that you don't know the customs. They don't have culture. They see and think that you have bad intentions."

"Oh, no," you say.

"Leticia said that you did not have bad intentions."

"No."

"That's all a mother worries about."

"I have no bad intentions," you say.

She offers you fruit and water, but you refuse. You apologize again, and explain that you are expected elsewhere. Before you go, however, you ask her permission to visit with Leticia.

"Oh, yes," she says proudly. "You can sit in the yard and talk. What a wonderful young man."

You visit Leticia nearly every day over the following weeks. You visit in front of her house, she on a stool and you in a hammock. The first time she hardly speaks, and you guess it is nervousness. But it never changes. You eat mangoes and while away the time by pulling strings from your teeth.

When you aren't with her, you spend time answering questions in the bar about the United States. You are asked the prices of cars and televisions, of houses and food. The men often say they want to sneak into the country "under water," as they say, work for a few months and return rich.

Leticia always has a radio on. When a love song plays, she sings the words to you as if the tune rings straight from her heart.

"Do you love me?" she asks once.

"We just met. It's hard to know. I mean, do you love me?"

"Oh, yes! At first sight."

"But we hardly talk."

"Talk to me, then," she says, and settles herself in, ready for you to pour out ... what?

"Uh, well," you say. "What do you want to do?"

"Talk."

"No, I mean in life."

"I don't know."

"You don't have plans?"

"I want to leave."

"To go where?"

"The United States," she says.

There, she discovers a space for communication and asks you how much your trip cost, how long it took, what it is like to fly in an airplane, if a sea of clouds swells and bucks like a sea of water, and how much money you earn. When the conversation peters out, you peel a mango. You move forward to get more comfortable; she misunderstands and leans forward with open mouth to kiss you.

And so it is each time you visit: You barely speak, she sings love songs to you, you sit and, finally, begin kissing. Once she scratches the outline of your penis with her fingernail until it becomes erect. You ask her to make love several times. She always says no. You try to arrange a way to be alone with her, but she says that it would be impossible. You sit silently. You kiss. Your anxious hands can hold her young breasts, can caress all of her lean body through her thin cotton dresses.

One time, she asks for your address back home. You give it to her and write down hers.

"But you have to write," she says. Her dark eyes glimmer in the sunlight.

"I promise," you say.

Dogs of Clowerston

Omar Castañeda shot the dog point blank. Earlier he had ripped the plastic wrapping from around a thawed chicken and slid the gun barrel in and out of the neck cavity. The inside of the gun remained clean. In an identical motion—that is, the black barrel slipping back and forth inside the moist opening—he shot through the dog's mouth. Before the blast, he remembered reading that cormorants of Lake Tayasal peck the eyes of fish too large to eat. The fish die slowly with no eyes. Nearby owls also peck the eyes of ocellated turkeys while they sleep in branches.

The sun had come up, but the drizzly morning left an interminable dusk. He left the shattered body and walked home through the alleyways.

Lori was still asleep, so Omar opened the bedroom closet and quietly lowered the blue suitcase. She had told him not to wake her. He fingered the letter hidden underneath. Lori's breathing didn't change, her body remaining soft and pale in sleep. But instead of reading the letter again, he stared at a ball of dust in the corner of the closet, then he put the suitcase back so that Lori or God could swear it had not been disturbed. Kato, their beagle, pattered up the stairs and looked at him.

He believed one can look at dogs, into their eyes, and feel an understanding. That's a romanticism he liked. Often, early in the evening, in the open fields between Clowerston's sandstone buildings, with trees fanned against the bruise-colored sky, just saying "yes" to the world, quietly and breathlessly, carried such unambiguous meaning. Truth.

He made breakfast for himself, dropping an egg and sausage into Kato's bowl before sitting down to eat. They ate together, looking across the room at each other. After washing the few dishes, he sat down to read the *Scientific American* he had taken from the library. Reading new journals or new books before anyone else was a right he claimed for himself as assistant librarian. Miss Cordon, the head librarian, used to complain about his taking the items home before proper cataloguing, but he continued without a word spoken in defense or comment whatsoever until she never mentioned it again.

The phone rang. The bedroom phone was set louder than the one in the living room. Omar let it ring four times before answering.

"Did I wake you?" the voice asked.

"No."

"Is Lori awake?" Omar sipped his coffee. Miriam Blanchard should know that Lori would not be awake.

"No."

"Could you have her call in as soon as she's awake?"

"What is it?"

"We're short again. We need her to do another double shift tonight."

"Isn't it too soon or something?"

"Just have her call, okay?"

"Yeah," he said. Lori would not object to working two double shifts in a row. She never complained. Even on a Saturday.

He wrote the message on a piece of note paper and ripped a square of tape. Upstairs, he put the note on the mirror of her vanity, then picked her clothes up from the floor. He carefully folded the jeans and a bright red blouse. He glanced over at her naked body, then set her shoes upright in the closet.

Downstairs, he locked the door behind him and walked into town. At this hour on a Saturday, very few people stirred from their homes. He walked leisurely, taking deliberate note of each trimmed lawn he passed. Their house was near the bottom of a cul-de-sac, so Omar passed seven houses before reaching the main street cutting through town. Most of the lawns were immaculate. His needed work.

From the corner, it was about a mile to the library. The greater city stretched eight blocks beyond that. It was a town he appreciated only after several years in Indianapolis. Clowerston grew a commuter's distance from that city and remained a basically rural small town. The tallest and newest building in Clowerston, headquarters for Midland Electronics, rose only eight stories. The older business buildings, with their beige sandstone sides, reached half as high. The Morrison Hotel only reached five stories. He liked it that Clowerston would never be a city of any real size. The town stopped abruptly within country-walking distances and disappeared into barely undulating fields where walnuts and maples commanded the sky; cornfields stretched like lakes to wooded horizons. At night, the dull white skylight of Indianapolis could be seen to the northwest.

Omar walked an extra two blocks out of his way so that he could pass a wild section of east Clowerston. The sloping fields, with their clustered elms and Douglas firs, had never been cleared there, so that a half-mile swath encroached on the town. Omar walked there to hear the sweep of birds in the mornings.

This time, he stopped at Gwynne's before going on to the library. It was a well lit place in the morning, where Clowerston's police ate breakfast and flirted with the waitresses. By mid-afternoon, however, the smell of beer kicked in. At night, Gwynne's was a bar.

He entered and waved at Betsy Simpson and her husband. He envied them. It had been nearly a month since Lori had gotten up so they could eat together. He ordered coffee and sat at a table by the bar so that he could see the entire room. Omar got his coffee and drank slowly. The library would not open for two hours.

Omar opened a morning newspaper left on the neighboring table and scanned the pages for mention of dogs. There were two articles. One was the report of yet another dog killed in Clowerston. A black lab had been poisoned in the alleyway behind the library. Omar looked over at Betsy. The other article was in the opinion section. An easy denouncement of the person or persons who would be so sick as to kill dogs. Omar read through the classifieds, then started the crossword puzzle. He did not notice Betsy's husband leaving, nor Betsy approaching, so that when she stood beside him and spoke, he started. Betsy chuckled about it.

"Sorry." She sat down. "Thought I'd join you. John went to work."

"Oh."

"Anything interesting in the paper?"

"No," he said, pushing it toward Betsy. "Want some coffee?"

"No, I'm coffeed out." A laugh opened her doughy face. "I don't see how you drink so much without going bananas. If I drink more than two cups, I'm a damn chicken with its head cut off."

"I guess I'm used to it. Maybe it's my age."

Betsy giggled. "Naw, you're not old."

"Thank you."

Sarah, the waitress, refilled Omar's cup.

"How far did you go?"

Omar didn't quite understand. "The crossword, you mean?"

"Yes."

"Oh, barely started. You want it?"

"No." She stroked the water glass, wiping the moisture so that it ran in beads. "Unless you want to do it."

"You mean together?"

"Yeah, let's do it."

"I don't know."

"You're so smart, we'd finish in no time." She slid her chair nearer to his. "Besides, we have lots of time to kill."

"Well, I suppose." He sipped his coffee, then opened the paper.

"How many cups have you had?"

"About four, I guess."

Betsy shook her head.

"All right," he said.

Omar read down the clues while Betsy read over his arm. Neither one said anything for a moment, so Omar read one-across.

"Three letter word for 'formerly.' "

Betsy stared into Omar's face as she struggled with the clue. Her lips were pressed together. Omar waited. He took another sip of coffee. He looked into Betsy's eyes. She stared seriously. He wondered if she was really thinking about the clue or about cookies or flea-markets or making love to her husband. How did they have sex? He picked up his pen.

"'Nee'," he said.

"Oh, for crying out loud! Who would know that?"

"I don't know," he said.

"Let's not work it. Who would know things like that?"

He folded the paper.

"By the way," she said, "I need that Scientific American you took. Some people have already asked for it. Mostly high-schoolers working on papers."

"I'm impressed," he said flamboyantly. "Intelligence is up!"

"What're you reading about now?"

"About a certain narcotic in a cat's brain."

"Yeah?"

"Yep. Even lions secrete it." He tapped on the table. "It's great stuff."

"I don't see how high school kids can read that stuff. It's so hard."

Omar drained his cup and motioned for Sarah.

"That'll give you nightmares," Betsy said.

"Maybe," he said, accepting another cup. "Thanks, Sarah. I've been having some odd dreams lately." He tore open a packet of sugar and tapped out half the contents. He set the packet on the table as if it were a fragile and heavy thing.

"Like what?"

"Just odd ones."

"Tell me. I always like to hear other people's dreams."

Omar chuckled. "You must be about the only one who does. I don't even like telling them."

"Tell me," she said, pushing the small of her back against the chair, pouting in her chubby-faced way.

"People say they like to hear dreams, but they really don't."

"Please," she said.

"They're nothing, really. It's just that they've been extremely realistic. They're about people I know. They're so real that I wake up and can't tell if I was just dreaming or if I did the dream."

"*Did* the dream?"

"I dream very ordinary things."

"Tell me," she said.

"Like you: I dreamed that we were in the library and you came out of the stacks and asked to borrow five dollars. You said you needed it to pay for something that had to do with your kids, but that you'd forgotten your purse at home. When I awoke, I couldn't tell if I had dreamed about something that really happened or if it was all just a dream. And even days later, when I thought about the dream, I still didn't know if

you had borrowed the money. Just today I wondered about
it."

"I didn't."

"Well, I've been having dreams like that."

"Does it bother you? I mean, you believe me that I didn't
borrow the money, right? Because I didn't."

"Of course, I believe you. But I had to realize the chances
of you leaving your purse at home. No, the dreams bother me
because I can't remember if I owe money, if people owe me
money, if I was supposed to meet someone, or call someone...
things like that."

"Maybe you're losing your mind." She wiggled her fingers
eerily.

Omar smiled.

"I'm amazed that you can remember your dreams."

"Don't you?"

"Not usually." She looked for a moment into Omar's face,
then said challengingly, "Tell me about a dream you had last
night."

"You're kidding!"

"No, come on."

"Forget it."

"Come on!"

"All right." He finished his coffee and collected his
thoughts, and ordered another. "I dreamed that Lori was living in a tall apartment building. It was too big for Clowerston, but I don't know where it is. For some reason, I was
working with the fire department. Her building caught fire.
Sometimes, the building looked real nice, like a city high-rise,
but other times the building changed into a kind of tenement.
The fire burned through the bottom floors, licking up the
sides of the building and turning everything black. Lori lived
on the floor just above the flames. She was leaning out of the
window, screaming for me to help her.

"I arrived in a huge fire truck filled with all sorts of people. Then the sidewalks filled with people from all parts of the

world: Chinese, Arabs, Mexicans... Once we get there, though, the truck disappears. Each of us has a fire hose which we plug into the building opposite Lori's. She is still screaming for me to rescue her, but I realize that my hose won't reach far enough. I've taken the wrong hose from the truck and now it's gone. I turn away because I think that she'll die, but I hear other firemen saving her. Lori tries to tell everyone that it was me who saved her, that she would have died if it weren't for me, but I turn away from her and from everyone else because already she seems dead to me."

Betsy turned up her nose. "Sounds like you made it up, you know?"

"It does, doesn't it? Pretty Freudian."

"Well, I don't remember my dreams."

"Lately," Omar continued, "I've been dreaming about the dogs."

"Ooh," she said, her eyes squinting angrily. Betsy tightened her fist. "Only a nut would do that."

"It's incredible. I'm worried about Kato." Omar frowned. "At least they're all strays. He's actually getting rid of nuisances, you know."

"That's disgusting."

"I don't mean it's good or anything, but just to look on the bright side. The dogs were strays. Clowerston does have a problem with them."

"But to kill them?"

"Well... He's crazy. A psychopath or something."

"You want to work the puzzle some more?"

"No." Betsy wiped the table with a sweep of her hand.

"Have some coffee?"

"No." She looked at the remaining customers.

Omar drummed the tabletop with his fingers. "Maybe we should just go set things up."

"Okay." Betsy stood to leave, then sat again as Omar pulled money from his pocket to pay. "Maybe Cordon's there."

Outside, the mottled sky kept Clowerston dank. They walked the few blocks in silence.

Miss Cordon was there. She opened the door for them, even though Omar had a key. Omar went into his office, where a stack of letters and forms from subscription agencies awaited him. Betsy began her morning search for stray books and magazines left on tables and shelves.

Omar worked through hours of forms until he thought that Lori would be up and ready for her "breakfast." He called, but the phone was busy. He called four more times in the next fifteen minutes and each time the phone beeped busy. When he finally dialed through, Lori spoke as if she had just awakened, yawning and breathing huskily into the phone.

"Uh-huh?"

"I called, but the phone was busy."

"Must have misdialed. What's the weather like?"

"Damp. It rained last night. There's no sun, really."

"Figures."

"Did you get the note I left you?"

"No. What's it say?"

"Miriam called and wants you to work another double tonight."

"Jesus Christ! Another one?"

"Maybe you can tell them you already had plans."

"No, I'd better not."

"It's up to you."

"No, I'd better go in. They're always so short."

"They should fire What's-her-name."

"Yeah. Thanks, Hon. Wait a second." Omar heard her light a cigarette and blow the smoke out with force.

"How about lunch?" he asked at the end of her exhale.

"Are you off?"

"No, but I can take an hour or so to eat with you. Things're slow as usual."

"When should I get you?"

"In an hour?"

"Okay."

One hour and forty-five minutes after the telephone conversation, Omar saw the silver Oldsmobile come around the
corner. Lori smiled from behind the wheel. As soon as Omar
sat down, he leaned to kiss her cheek.

"Hi-ya," she said.

She wore a western blouse and Levi skirt. Her curled hair
bunched in ringlets across her shoulders. Omar reached out
and wrapped the longer strands around his finger. "You look
great," he said.

"Where should we go?"

"It's up to you."

"You decide, for once."

Omar looked at her outfit again, noticing the tan boots.
"Mcdonald's?"

Lori smirked.

He rolled the window down an inch. "The Wild Turkey?"

She patted his leg. "Good idea, Babe."

Lori glanced toward the Morrison Hotel. A large red car
had just pulled in and a tall man with a briefcase stepped out.
A woman in a white formal dress stood waiting to greet him.

"You know them?" Omar asked.

"Who? Oh, no."

"Maybe by night's end."

They drove through the center of town. Lori's smoking
was more relaxed than usual. She let the smoke drift from
between her teeth in near breathlessness, or let thin clouds
brush over the dashboard. She watched everything that
moved outside. She seemed pleased. They waited at another
stop light. An African American walked into the crosswalk.
Lori turned her head just slightly to watch the man. Omar
looked at Lori, who smiled at him. The light changed.

"Do you suppose it's true that Blacks are good in bed?"

"Do you think Blacks make better lovers? African Ameri-
cans."

"Jesus Christ, Omar, you're an idiot sometimes."

She threw out her half-smoked cigarette, then opened her purse to take out another one. She flicked her lighter several times before keeping it lit.

Omar waited through the edge of silence. "When do you have to be at the hotel?"

"Same as always," she said curtly.

"That gives us a little more than an hour."

"We'll eat fast."

It was a short and silent drive remaining. The restaurant on the far side of town advertised a special on western style ribs and cornbread.

"That sounds good," Omar said, pointing to the sign.

She didn't respond. She turned into the parking lot and stopped.

The inside walls of the restaurant were made to look constructed of old barnwood, the dining tables to look like chopping blocks coated with thick plastic. Embedded in the plastic were confederate coins and postcards of the wild west shows of Buffalo Bill, Calamity Jane and others. The waitresses all wore cowboy hats and frilled waistcoats.

Lori rolled her eyes.

"Watcha half, pardner?" she said when the hostess left.

Omar smiled.

"Maybe I should go into the restaurant business."

They ordered drinks first, then looked through the leather-bound menus. Omar rubbed the embossed turkey on the cover while watching Lori read and surreptitiously glance about the room. A waitress brought coffee for Omar and a Tom Collins for Lori.

Lori lit another cigarette. She rested her chin on the back of her right hand and rested it in the palm of the hand holding the cigarette. In this position, to smoke was the slightest of gestures. She lifted her chin an inch, drew her fingers in so the butt touched her lips and sucked. The exhaled smoke fanned across her hand, or shot straight to the ceiling in a

thin stream when she lifted her chin up high. Her eyes followed every moving person, checked every table within view.

"Still looking?" he said carefully.

She dropped her hands to the table. "What?"

"There're a lot of men here today."

"For Christ's sake, Omar, don't start."

"Sorry."

"Why don't we just sit here and have a good time."

They sipped their drinks quietly. A young man came to
fill their water glasses. Lori thanked him. Omar picked up the
newly filled glass and drank.

"Is he good-looking?"

Lori sighed. "What is it with you?"

"Just a question."

"Right!"

"It is."

"Do you want me to go through life with blinders? You
want me to see only you or only what's in front of me? You're
insanely jealous."

"Observant."

"Observant? And I can't be?"

Omar smiled thinly.

"You can look anywhere you want, but I can't. Is that
right?" She jabbed out her cigarette. "Men are all the same!"

"Why do you always make the issue larger than what it
is?"

"Well, what the hell is the issue? That I'm a whore? That
I can't keep my eyes off of men? That all I want to do is have
sex?"

"No."

"You want me to confess that I'm a whore?"

"No." He hunched his shoulders. "Keep your voice down."

"Then why do you have to ruin our lunch?"

"I'm sorry," he said, looking away from tables around
them.

Lori stared blankly at the pictures in their booth.

"I'm sorry," Omar said.

She stared blindly.

Omar ripped the paper napkin beside his plate. "I'm sorry," he said. He balled up the paper between his fingers. "It was stupid. A stupid display of emotion. I was out of line."

"You jump to conclusions," she said. "You're always assuming things about me. It's like you don't trust me, like you look for reasons to hate me. Why the fuck stay with me, then?"

"Sh!" he said. "Look, I'm sorry."

Lori swallowed her drink.

"Let's talk about something else."

"Let's!" She pulled another cigarette from her pack.

Omar sipped the coffee, then his water. He watched the smoke pour from Lori's lips. Lori stared bluntly at him.

"I talked to Betsy today about dreams," Omar said. "Want to hear about a dream I had?"

She moved the ashtray closer.

Omar spread his hands flat against the table. "I dreamed that I poisoned a labrador and left it behind the library. I dreamed that I was the one killing all the dogs in town because there was this darkness, this monster stuck in my chest."

Lori looked at him, stared at him. "You're insane, you know that?"

"It's true," he said.

II.

Omar awoke later than usual the next morning. He tried to remember when Lori had come in, but couldn't. He had slept very soundly for once. He went quietly down the stairs to let Kato out and to make coffee. By the time the water boiled, Kato was back and whimpering to get in. They ate breakfast together, quietly so Lori would not wake up. She would sleep very late after two double shifts in a row.

Omar cleared the dishes and walked outside with his cup. A pair of robins called in the oak tree by the city lot. The female was probably already pregnant, he thought. They would guard the tree carefully, even hectoring Kato if he came too close. Omar admired the robin's habit of luring danger away from the nesting area. Robins, he thought, approached the habits of killdeers. Though far less dramatic. A robin would scurry away and wait for the attention of the intruder, calling out if necessary. And when the intruder followed, the robin would lead further out. Once the little ones hatched, the female would help the male in the ploy. If another robin ventured too close, the couple would hop up and flutter challengingly until the boundary was unmistakably clear.

But the best defense of home, he thought, was the strong offense of the cuckoo's. By destroying the eggs of other birds and placing its own egg in the nest, the cuckoo saved itself the burden of the whole relationship.

Omar tossed down the rest of his coffee and tied Kato to a post in the backyard. Inside, he wiped the table and swept the kitchen floor. He noticed that the floor would need to be waxed soon. Halfway up the stairs, he moved around to re-evaluate the sheen of the floor.

Omar coughed next to Lori. Her eyelids were still. He sat beside her head and touched her shoulder. He stood and said her name in a normal voice. He asked her if she would be working late again. She made no reply. He told her that he got a raise at work. She did not move. He slid open the closet door and lowered the blue suitcase. Now there were two letters underneath. He took the new letter into the bathroom.

His face flushed as he read the letter, and when he finished, he unzipped his pants and urinated. Then he leaned over the sink and stared into his own eyes.

Kato barked.

Quickly, he put the letter and suitcase back. He stood over Lori again. Her mouth was partly open, the pillow damp from breathing. Omar opened her underwear drawer and rummaged through these clothes she never wore. He opened another drawer and searched. Omar searched through all five of her drawers.

He leaned breathlessly over the chest of drawers and bowed his head. Directly in front of him, Lori's jewelry box held what he sought. He lifted the small tape measure key chain from among the necklaces and read the words "Fran's Goodyear" written in red letters. Slowly, he pulled the tape inch by inch until he saw the bright red heart drawn with magic marker. He licked his little finger and ran it down the concave tape. The groove was just the right width to accommodate the very tip of his finger. As his moistened finger passed over the length of tape, a red shadow smeared a quarter of an inch from the drawn heart. Omar stared into his eyes in the mirror above the dresser, then dropped the tape measure back into Lori's jewelry box.

He touched himself to erection as he crawled next to Lori. She shrugged when he opened her legs. Lori opened her eyes and groaned. "No, Babe," she said. Omar moved slowly inside her. She placed her hand against his neck and spoke slowly. "Please, Omar, I'm too tired." He quickened his movements. Lori sighed loudly, and gave him more freedom. Her head fell sleepily to one side. Omar pushed feverishly inside her for a minute or two, then tightened in orgasm. Lori smiled up with her eyes closed. "That was nice," she said, her eyes still closed, her head lolling. "That was nice." He shrank out of her, and she rolled onto her side. "Stay with me," she said.

Omar slowed his breathing, feeling the pulse rack at his temples, and watched Lori fall back to sleep. Exhausted, he drifted off without even being aware of falling asleep.

Some time later, he awoke with a sense of urgency, hoping to capture the fleeting details of a dream. While he searched for paper, he pictured Betsy sitting in Gwynne's. He wrote what he could remember: crickets in the wild swath of Clowerston, chirping incessantly; he threw pebbles into a night sky and watched a bat swing down, then dart upward from the decoy. The bat snarled at a red and white moon like an angry cat, its face leonine, mane-rich.

III.

"Another dog was found poisoned last night," Lori said.

Omar rubbed his forearms beneath the kitchen table. Lori folded the paper. She joined him at the table.

"I have to work a couple of hours," he said.

"Okay."

"You're not working tonight?"

"I thought I'd eat with Miriam tonight, then have a few drinks. Maybe we'll go to a movie."

Omar wiped the table, then threw the cloth into the sink. Lori sighed.

"What's the big deal?" she asked.

"Last week you worked two doubles in a row—Friday and Saturday, at that—and this week you've already done one double."

"So?"

"When you're not working late, all you want to do is sleep or watch television."

"Okay," she said, "and now I want to do something else."

"Going out with Miriam isn't exactly what I had in mind."

"Look, Omar, I'm going out with her tonight. We can do something tomorrow."

"Are you sure you have the night off?"

"No, but if I do, we'll do something. I promise."

Omar stepped to the cabinets for lunch plates. "When will you know about tomorrow?"

"Tomorrow."

He set the plates down and folded napkins beside them.

"Sit down," she said. "I'll get everything."

"It's done."

"I'll serve, then. Just sit down."

"I suppose you won't be here when I get back."

"Probably not, Babe."

"I see."

"I'll do the dishes," she said.

They ate while listening to the three-o'clock news. When they finished, Omar helped Lori with the dishes. She needed to take a shower and get fixed up, she said. While she showered, Omar looked through her dresser.

The week before, so many more letters had arrived that Lori took them from beneath the suitcase and hid them in her underwear. Omar felt elated the first day when he saw the letters missing. He thought it was all over, but then remembered the urgency of the last one and looked through her clothes. There, he found a pack of seven letters. The pain he felt on reading them was different after the giddiness of believing this affair over. He felt a dull throb in his chest, an ache behind his ribs, not the usual frenetic beating of his heart and the constriction at his groin.

Now, he felt only sadness, as if the letters were addressed to him and spoke, instead, of the discouragements of close friends, of their struggles for some happiness. Omar counted the letters, listening to the sound of the shower. There were no new ones, so he put the packet back. There had been no new letters for the past three days.

It made sense, he suddenly thought, that she would go somewhere else. If he continually thought she was going out on him, then it made sense that she would actually do it. She might as well. Omar sat on the bed, where Lori had set out a long dress and white shoes. He hated himself for sneaking through her clothes and jewelry, for shooting that dog, for imagining every man pawing his wife.

"I'm leaving," he called out. "I have to go."

"Goodbye, Honey," she sang back.

The library was closed to the public, but Miss Cordon had asked Omar and Betsy to do special work that afternoon. A new collection of journals on the fauna of Australia and Madagascar required immediate cataloguing. They worked in Omar's office, where the glass partitions reflected their faces and bodies.

They hunched over the paperwork like plump monkeys. Betsy would occasionally stop and groan, then rise to drink from the fountain, or complain about using the restroom too often while moving to use it. Omar couldn't blame her. The work was monotonous and boring to begin with. Ordinarily, Omar would peruse most items he catalogued. He was too much the avid reader. He would do it leisurely, but with so many to catalogue by morning, there was no time for it.

When they neared the end of the task, it was already dark. Betsy complained loudly, saying that it wouldn't be so bad, but they had to return to work the next morning. And why didn't Cordon help out?

"Who knows what she's doing?" he said.

"Why don't you come with John and me to Gwynne's for a beer?" Betsy said. "Just a quickie."

Omar cleaned up the paperwork strewn over the tables and discovered another complete listing beneath a thick computer run. Betsy said "shit" under her breath as if she were trying to blow the word down her blouse. Omar shook his head. "You go ahead," he said. "I'll do these and meet you later, if you're still there."

"Are you sure? I can stay and help."

"No," he said. "I'll finish up in no time. There aren't that many, really."

He was wrong. The last series took him longer than he had expected. He worked another two hours with the cataloguing, regretting that he had spoken so soon. He knew that Betsy and her husband would be gone. He decided to take a short walk and then get a beer by himself. Attracted by the lights on the main street, he walked further into town. An old sports car, full of screaming teen-agers, sped past. The boys inside called out drunkenly, catcalling and ridiculing Omar as he walked quietly down the pavement, minding his own business. He wondered if young lemurs ever harassed old and dying males, if any species of animal ever weeded out the weaker ex-patriarchs. For a moment, he saw a young girl's face peer at him through the darkened rear window of the car. In that face, he remembered that virtually all species attack their older members. The old males weakened, hollowed without a fight or they died in bloody heaps. He waved at the ghostly face.

Omar turned down an alleyway behind the Morrison Hotel. Lori's car was parked in its usual place. It irritated him to think that she might have been called in to work because of that young What's-Her-Name. They should fire her, he thought. Too many people don't take their responsibilities seriously enough. The old can work, by God. They don't waste their time.

He jabbed the bell behind the hotel. The overhead floodlight cast his shadow into the darkness beyond, so that only his body lay outlined on the concrete, his head lost in the nightshade beyond. He stood there longer than usual, picturing the path Lori would have to take from the secured telephone room, down the hallway, and to the outside door. After the murder of an operator in Washington during a robbery, the management of the Morrison Hotel decided to get special security measures for the switchboard. The operators controlled the entire hotel security system, as well as guarding the safe and security boxes.

There was a shift in color across the spy-hole of the door. A bolt slid back and Frank, the electronics technician, smiled out.

"Come on in, champ," he said.

"Is Lori here?"

"Yeah."

"Is she busy?"

"Don't know," he said, and turned down the hallway.

"So, you're working nights these days," Omar said.

"Yep."

"Have you been doing it lately?"

Frank stopped and turned toward him. "Yeah," he said. "I've been doing it lately. How about you?"

"What? Oh, I see. No, I mean have you been working nights lately?"

"About a month."

Frank turned into the back room where he worked. His broad shoulders seemed to brush both sides of the doorway.

Omar knocked at the exchange.

Janis, the young operator, opened up. Lori sat on the large console, her legs crossed at the ankle. Her white dress hung just below her knees. Miriam sat on the couch beside her.

"What are you doing here?"

"Out walking. I saw your car, so I knocked."

Lori and Miriam exchanged glances.

"What are you doing here?"

"Mr. Morrison called Miriam and said that they needed someone to work late." Lori pointed at Janis. "She's leaving soon and can't stay, so I'm the one they want."

Miriam rubbed at a streak on her high-heeled shoes.

"It ruins your night out," Omar said.

"There's not much happening, anyway," Miriam said.

Janis answered a call, switching it to the proper room quickly.

Omar put his hands in his pockets. "I'll see you in the morning."

Miriam glanced at Lori. "Are we going to meet for breakfast?" she asked.

"Oh, yeah," Lori said. "Since we didn't go out tonight, we were going to have breakfast together." She stood and touched Omar's arm. "Is that all right, Babe?"

"Sure, why not?" He waited to see if he would be invited to join them.

Lori looked at Miriam. "We won't be long, will we?"

"No, I don't think so."

"Darn," Lori said, turning to Omar, "but you'll be going to work so I won't see you until the afternoon."

"Looks that way."

Lori pouted.

"I guess I'll go."

"I'll walk you to the door." She turned to Miriam. "Be right back."

In the hallway, Omar hissed in his throat. "They should fire that girl."

"Janis? She's nice. Just young, that's all."

They stopped by the front door.

"Do you want me to get some clothes for you or something?"

"Don't bother." She stroked her thigh and tilted her hip seductively. "I'll just be dressed to kill and no one will see."

"Hm."

"Why so blue?"

Omar reached for her waist. "I miss you."

"Ah, Babe," she said. "I'm sorry." She put her arms around his neck and kissed him. "Tomorrow, I'll be home, I think. Kiss me."

He did, and ran his hands down her back. The silkiness of the dress drew his fingers down across her hips. She wore no panties.

"Ooh," she said.

"I want you."

Her voice got husky. "Hold that thought for tomorrow."

"It's been too long."

She pushed him back. "You'd better go, Sweetie."

Omar looked up to see Frank smiling by a doorway, leaning against the frame with his arms crossed. Frank dropped his arms and stepped toward them.

"Oh, hi," Lori said, drawing away from Omar. "He's just leaving."

"Walking him to the door, I see."

"Yep." She reached out and stroked Omar's chin. "See you later, Hon."

"Don't worry," Frank said, stepping in front of Omar. "I'll lock up behind you."

Lori disappeared down the hallway.

IV

Betsy and her husband had already left Gwynne's by the time Omar arrived. He sat at the bar and ordered a beer. The patrons were mostly young men and a few women. Only two men sat at the bar. Omar eased up on the stool between them, with a vacant chair on either side. The older face on his right seemed familiar. Recently in the library, he supposed. He nodded to the man, who returned his own terse acknowledgment. Omar knew the bartender frequently bussed tables for lunch and, sometimes, even for breakfast. He was a thin man with an eye that appeared half-blind. A red semicircle covered half of his left pupil.

"I haven't seen much of you at night," the bartender said.

"I don't drink much."

"Sure slurp up the coffee, though."

Omar laughed. "Yeah, that's my vice."

"So long as you got one. So, what'll you have?"

He ordered a draft and, when it came, Omar wanted to ask the man how in the world he could work so many shifts and maintain a respectable contact with his family, but the bartender walked off to wipe things beneath the counter.

He could see some of the room through the mirror behind the bar. A large man wearing a leather motorcycle cap clutched a girl in the far corner almost directly behind Omar. The man had one muscular arm draped over the girl's shoulder, the other arm rested on the table and curved to encircle her. She was small enough to rest in the pouch of his arms, a pouch into which he frequently dipped his head with a guttural laugh that made Omar feel like he was being talked about. With the man's head up and periscopic about, the girl would kiss his neck. Even in the darkness of the bar, Omar could see the shadow of beard on the guy's face. He wondered if the sharpness of stubble against her lips was part of the attraction. That small pain.

The familiar face next to him ordered another beer. Omar took a sip and eye-measured the remains. He would have another, he thought. Omar downed the rest.

"I'll have one," he said loudly enough for the bartender and the familiar face to hear.

The face nodded. "You work at the library."

"Yes."

"Quiet work. Not like where I work."

"Oh?" Omar was glad for the conversation.

"Wish I could work somewhere quiet."

He saw that the man's eyes were glassy.

"I get noise all the time," the face continued. "Damn machines never give you a break. Running all the time. The doctor says my ears are shot. You think I get any compensation for that?"

"Where do..."

"And the kids need this damn thing and that damn thing. I ain't even got money for them. How the hell am I supposed to take care of my ears?"

Omar shrugged. He raised his glass to his lips.

"You know how much it costs to see a doctor? Too damn much, that's how much!"

"You're right."

"There's no big deal about ears, anyway." The face rubbed his forehead, then laughed. "It's like your prick. Once it's gone, just forget it. Don't think about it again." The man laughed, then tried to drown his laughter in a gulp of beer.

Omar sipped his.

"You got a wife?" the man asked with sudden sobriety.

"Yes."

The man gazed into his glass like he hadn't heard.

Omar checked the mirror. The leather-capped man and his woman friend were gone. He wondered briefly if he had imagined them. The man on Omar's other side put money on the bar and left with a friendly nod to him and to the familiar face.

"Be good," the face called out.

The departing man waved without looking back. Omar finished his beer and got up to go.

"Let me buy you one," the face said, raising his glass.

"I don't know. Two's about my limit."

Omar shrugged.

"Hell, it's free," the face said.

Omar tapped the bottom of his glass against the bar.

"Bar-keep," the face said. "Two more."

"Thanks."

"Forget it. What the hell's your name?"

"Omar Castañeda."

"That's a fucking name." He stretched to meet hands. "My name's Ernie."

"Glad to meet you, Ernie."

Ernie nodded drunkenly. "You're not an Arab, are you? I mean with a name like that."

"No."

"So where did you get a fucking name like that?"

"I'm Guatemalan."

"No shit? You sure don't look it."

Omar took a drink. "Just my luck, I guess."

"Say," Ernie said, "do you drink whiskey there, Oscar?"

"I'll pass, thanks."

"Yeah, I suppose I don't need that either." Ernie closed his eyes and rubbed his temples.

Omar watched through the mirror. Ernie's head swayed just inches above his glass. After nearly a minute, he raised his head abruptly and caught Omar staring.

Ernie raised his eyebrows. "My wife says I drink too much. Says all I do is drink."

Omar lowered his gaze.

Ernie stood suddenly. "Sorry," he said. "I got to go. You got to go when you say shit like that." He put money on the bar, too much for what Omar had seen him drink. "I got to go."

Ernie brushed against a woman near the door and continued on without apologizing. He pulled the door, then pushed it open.

The bartender shrugged.

"I guess I'll go, too," Omar said.

"Finish your beer. It's free."

When he finished, Omar stood, and wavered for an instant.

He welcomed the fresh air against his face. For a second, he thought he might become sober, but the deadened feeling came back quickly to his forehead. He stopped by a drugstore on the way home with the hope that it would be open. Instead, he found himself staring through the darkened store window at a newspaper just inside, staring dead at the front page account of another poisoned dog. Number ten, it said in large print. It was the same dog Lori had noticed earlier. The paper quoted the disgust of the director of the city pound.

"There's probably a reason," Omar said aloud, then turned to see if anyone had heard him. The street was empty up and down for blocks.

He continued toward his house, wishing for the sound of birds or the black shadowing of a bat, something magical...Lori's smile exploding in his eyes like stars. A dog scurried to the right of him, in an alleyway. Omar touched inside his coat pocket where he had carried the gun a week ago. He hurried behind houses and buildings to get to the wild section. Disappointingly, the sounds he wanted to hear were not there. He walked slowly home, thickly home.

Inside, he patted Kato's head and walked upstairs. His head and legs felt wooden, even when he reached for his gun in the back of the closet. He wiped the black barrel with a chamois cloth, then carefully removed all but one bullet. He spun the cylinder the way he had seen countless times in movies. He placed the extra bullets side by side in a cotton-lined box. He lifted one and held it so close that he could see his tiny reflection in the casing. He rubbed the slug in a circle around his forehead, feeling the smooth machined metal against his skin. Omar covered the bullets and returned them to the closet. Without a second thought he pointed the gun into the roof of his mouth and pulled the trigger.

Downstairs, he opened the refrigerator. He opened Tupperware bowls and old butter tubs of leftovers. He immersed his left hand into beef stew, then shook the excess liquid back into the tub.

"Kato!" he called, closing the refrigerator.

Omar stooped, reached out. "Come on, Kato," he said.

The dog whimpered. It kicked free of his hands.

"Sh, boy! It's all right. Here!"

He carried Kato into the back yard where he tied him to the post. "Goodbye, friend," he said, his voice like gauze in his mouth.

Omar walked through the back yards until he came to a fence. On the other side, his neighbor's dog growled quietly, slowly recognizing Omar's scent. Omar called to it. The dog pushed its snout through the chain link fence and sniffed Omar's hand. He let the animal lick his fingers, and guided the dog in this way to a corner of the yard where garbage cans stood like Canopic jars. Omar withdrew his gun, stuck three fingers through the fence. The dog's tongue slipped quickly and wetly between his fingers.

Omar knew the dog would understand what he was doing
if he thought too much. The dog would know his thoughts.
Everyone could read his thoughts if he wasn't careful. He
pointed the gun barrel through the links, letting it rest
against the paler metal. Close by, a click beetle righted itself.
Omar's stomach quivered. The dog's eyes were brown, the
sharp teeth glinted whitely behind dark lips. Bitter lips. But
then he had seen this dog before, he suddenly thought. Then
embarrassedly, losing the dream, he realized that, of course,
he had seen this dog before. It was his neighbor's dog. Fred's
dog. It wasn't a stray. "Of course," he whispered.

The dog stepped back and stared at Omar; its head tilted
to one side.

He had thought too long. Maybe there was still time. If
he could make his mind a complete blank, he thought. If he
could return to that obscure plane of mind where he did not
recognize the dog. He pointed directly at the dog's face, trying
to picture a darkness inside his mind, an emptiness that
clouded and comforted by its very emptiness. The animal
growled. Omar felt his stomach grumble with acidity. "I can't
freeze," he thought. "I can't freeze."

"Bang!" he shouted suddenly, unable to squeeze the trigger.

The dog scurried away from the abrupt noise, then
lunged back at the fence. The chain links chattered like cym-
bals. The violence of the attack so startled Omar that he fell
down amid the garbage cans. They clattered and set the dog
to leaping and barking in earnest.

A light snapped on. "Who's out there?" a voice called.

Omar tried putting the cans upright, but they fell against
each other. The dog kept lunging at the fence, rattling the
chain links. Barking. Barking.

"Who's there?" the voice shouted. "I have a gun!"

Omar scrambled up and ran headlong through the yards.
Behind him, not far enough behind him, not nearly far
enough, he heard a screen door smack against its wood frame.

V

Steve Hicks came into the library the next day. He said hello and asked for Betsy. Omar, who was checking books at the front desk, pointed to the stacks. Steve returned in several minutes and stood alongside him, casually glancing at the browsers. "So, how are you, Omar?" he asked.

Omar looked up. "Fine."

"Betsy's finding a book for me," Steve said, jerking a thumb toward the stacks. "You don't mind if I wait here for her, do you?"

He returned to his work. "No."

"I'm still on duty, but I figured I had enough time to get a book for my kid."

"What's she getting?"

Omar scribbled dates and figures on overdue notices.

"A science book." Steve put a hand on Omar's work. "You read science books, don't you?"

"Yes."

"I wish I knew more about science."

"Yes. It's helpful."

"I sure wish I knew about science. Maybe it would help me find out who's behind the dog poisonings."

"Oh, are you doing that?"

Steve sat on the desk and folded his arms. "It's not easy, though. I mean, who really cares about strays, anyway? You know what I mean?"

Omar tapped his pencil. "A lot of people care, I guess."

"I guess," Steve said. "It gets tricky, though." He picked up a pencil and read the writing on it. "You don't know anything about these dogs, do you?"

Omar looked at the stacks for Betsy. "No, I don't." He wondered if he had dreamed of telling Betsy, or if he had really told her. Suddenly, Steve sitting there in front of him asking about the dogs seemed all too familiar, too inevitable. He had seen this before.

"Maybe it's nothing, really," Steve said. "It doesn't hurt to ask people. After all, they're nothing but strays. It should probably be legal to kill them."

"No," Omar said, "I don't know anything about them."

"Actually, whoever's doing it is helping the city. Doing us all a favor. Don't tell anyone I said that, but we don't need a pack of wild dogs roaming the city. We have too many strays as it is."

Omar stared up. He did tell Betsy about the dog. They had been in Gwynne's solving a puzzle with her husband. They had stayed up all night. There had been chickens everywhere. Black chickens. And he had leaned forward and told Betsy about the dog. But why wasn't Steve arresting him?

Steve frowned. "You know," he said, "the thing is that only one dog was shot. The rest were poisoned. Sometimes you get somebody killing dogs out of an honest craziness, and then someone else joins the bandwagon and kills a dog or two just to see if they can do it. It's a milder thing, you know? It's the kind of person who's usually a real nice guy, like you or me, but maybe he's always wanted to kill a dog, or something. Some other guy is already doing it, so, hey, why not take the opportunity?"

"You can understand it then," Omar said. His hands felt heavy on the desk.

"I can't really blame someone like that. It's not like they're killing people. They're strays that would be killed at the pound sooner or later, anyway."

Omar thought he'd better not remember his neighbor's dog, picture its face. He wouldn't want Steve to know about that. Steve would be able to see what he was thinking.

Steve looked over his shoulder quickly, then put his face next to Omar's. "You have a gun, don't you?" he asked conspiratorially.

"What?

"You have a gun."

"Yes, I have a gun."

"You have a license for it?"

"Yes."

"When did you get it?"

"I worked two years as a security guard for Lilly in Indianapolis. After my service. I got a gun because the one they issued was too heavy."

Steve leaned back and spoke in a normal voice. "Seems like I remember hearing that."

Omar looked at the stacks. "What's taking Betsy so long?"

"I'm in no rush," Steve said.

"Maybe I should help her."

"Don't bother." Steve crossed his arms. "Yeah," he said, "we got a call last night about someone prowling around in your neighborhood."

Omar imagined himself reading under the tall lamp in the living room. He imagined the cream rug, the fireplace poker.

"I tell you what. I can probably excuse one stray dog being killed, but someone killing somebody's pet is different. Particularly with a gun."

"I didn't hear anything last night," Omar said.

"Happened around ten o'clock. I was watching television and drinking beer. What were you doing?"

"I was home."

"Watching TV?"

"No, I was reading."

"What were you reading?"

"A novel," Omar said.

"A science novel?"

"No, a Hemingway novel."

"What was the title?"

"For Whom the Bell Tolls."

Steve Hicks stared at Omar for a second, then he burst out laughing with undisguised disbelief.

Omar felt his face flush.

"Listen," Steve said firmly, "I'm looking for someone who's poisoning dogs. That's a psychosis we don't want here. And it's not odd for some poor sucker to join the bandwagon because of some weird need. But that's temporary." He stared hard at Omar. "Temporary! We hardly ever find out who does that sort of thing, but if he starts killing pets, that's a serious beginning. Firing a gun in the city is even more serious. You understand? We do not want that to happen again."

Omar nodded.

"Do you understand?"

"Yes," Omar said.

"I seriously hope you do. Now go and tell Betsy that I'll send my boy over here later."

Omar nodded.

Steve Hicks stood with his fingertips at the edge of the desk, fixing Omar with his eyes, then he left. Omar waited for the door to close behind him before rising to find Betsy in the stacks.

"What book?" she said. "He said that he wanted to speak with you in private. For me to leave you two alone."

Omar ran the heel of his palm across the back of the books, feeling the narrow ridges scrub across his flesh.

"Maybe I misunderstood," he said.

VI

Omar smiled at Kato. "It's over," he said. He grinned and rubbed Kato's head between his hands. He wanted to laugh out loud, but kept the laugh, like a secretive animal, in his throat. He grinned widely, foolishly.

Lori had left for the morning shift for the first time in many weeks. Omar rummaged through her dresser, through the closet and eagerly through every conceivable hiding place in the house. The letters were gone. The last letter, found four days earlier, had been cool. That night, he remembered, Lori had snuggled up to him in bed. She must have destroyed the letters while he slept. There was no other time, he thought.

Omar made a pot of coffee and mixed a batch of pancakes. He cracked an egg and dropped it onto Kato's dog food. The foolish animal in his throat kept churning, forcing Omar to smile and laugh quietly. Kato pushed against Omar's legs and wagged his tail every time Omar grinned.

"Okay, okay, boy," he said. "It's done."

While they ate, Lori called.

"Just wanted to say good morning," she said.

"Thank you," he said. "Thank you very much."

"You sound cheerful."

He chuckled.

"Is it nice out? I didn't notice."

"Well, sure, I guess." Omar walked to the window and pulled the curtain. It was partly sunny, with a stripe of sunlight flying across the lawn.

"Are you looking?" Lori asked.

"Yes. It looks great."

Omar heard her light a cigarette. "How about you?" he asked. "You doing okay?"

"Yeah. Just okay."

"Sorry."

"Why? It's not your fault."

"Sorry for you."

Lori blew smoke noisily. "You want to have lunch?"

"I can't."

"Why not?"

"I have extra work today."

"Please?"

"No thanks, Babe." Omar scratched Kato's head. "But why don't you pick me up after work and we'll eat?"

"Fine. What time?"

"Five."

Later, at three minutes to five, Lori drove up to the steps of the library and got out so that Omar could drive.

"Are you all right?" he asked.

"Yeah, sure." She slid next to him on the seat.

He pulled from the curb. "Where to?"

"I don't care."

"Wild Turkey?"

"If you want." Lori put her head on Omar's shoulder.

He rubbed his cheek against her hair. "You smell good. You seem soft, too. Are you tired?"

She kissed his shoulder. "I wish I could be soft for you all the time." She looked down at her lap.

When she lifted her head, Omar saw that her eyes were red. "Are you crying?"

"No."

He kissed her temple.

"Let's go home," she said.

"Are you all right?"

"I'm just tired." Lori sighed. "Maybe the late shifts've finally gotten to me. All that juggling."

"Maybe we won't have late shifts for a while."

Lori looked into Omar's face. Her eyes were red, her expression frozen as if as she were about to speak.

At home, Lori dipped her fingers inside Omar's hand and led him to the bedroom. She kissed him, undressed tiredly and threw her bra and panties onto the floor. Omar watched from the doorway. He waited for what she wanted.

"Lie down with me," she said. She pulled the sheet up to her chin.

Omar undressed and slipped in beside her. "Do you want to make love?"

Lori put her head on his chest. "No, I just want you to hold me."

He folded his arms over her back. He pressed his cheek tightly against her head, feeling the burning of his eyes. He didn't want them to be wet. No tears! No wet!

"Do you love me?" she asked.

"Yes," he said tightly.

Lori kissed his chest. She brushed his nipple with her fingernail. "I forget," she said, "how good you are. You love me for me, don't you?"

Omar combed her hair with his fingers.

"Even with your jealousy," she added, pressing deeper into his chest.

Downstairs, Kato's claws clicked on the kitchen floor. In the room, their nightstand clock ticked audibly.

"I had a strange dream the other night," Omar said.

She looked up into his eyes. She seemed to search in the light hidden there his dark pupils for a clue as to his mood.

He gently pushed her head down onto his chest. "It's an odd one. It might make you mad."

"Baby, don't. Please."

"It started with you buried up to your neck in sand by the sea."

"Do you have to?"

"There's an African boy standing beside you with a club you'd given him. He's swinging it like a golf club, but it isn't an ordinary golf club. It has a razor edge that will sever your neck. The flat face will send your head into the sea."

"God, Omar, please don't ..."

"See, you want him to do it. You asked him to do it. You're calm. In some way, this is penitence. But each time the boy swings, you yell 'eyes, eyes,' because the boy keeps missing and knocking sand into your face. Your face is so expressive. The boy's family and friends watch from red and white tents, but they get bored. Some of them leave. The boy keeps trying. One time, he has to whisk away sand from the pocket of your mouth.

"Behind him, there's a small parade of Africans nearing us. At first it looks like oil spreading over the sand. You see them, too, and get angry. The newcomers are carrying a lion.

You shout at them and the lion turns its head. I see the strong and youthful face and think that it is smiling.

"At first, you're very angry with them. You tell me that they're going to dismember the lion. They'll strip off the skin and eat the meat from the lion's head. You ask me if I remember your restaurant in Texas where you served meat not only from the lion's head, but from its entire body. You desperately want me to remember your achievement. 'I didn't waste anything!' you shout at them. Even then, you whisper sadly to me, you hated Africans for leaving the limbs of lions scattered on beaches.

"For some reason, I was living proof that your restaurant was actually decent and legitimate. And yet, I had done something that destroyed your good image. Most people had forgotten you, but because of what I had done, you were buried neck deep in the sand. I wanted the people in the tents to know the truth about you. That's why I did something terrible.

"Anyway, the boy swung again and missed. Suddenly, I realized that we weren't facing the sea. We had been looking landward, staring at the infinite sand. The slight rolls of windswept desert had fooled me into thinking of the sea. But when I turned to look at the ocean, I knew the sand and sea were equally beautiful, equally deadly.

"Well, I walked out over the rolling dunes and into the desert, trying to remember what it was that I had said or done to get you buried alive. I expected to hear your final scream coming from over the dunes. Like the waste of lion's meat, it all seemed so inevitable. But under the heat of the sun, you melted away. Everything—the tents, the Africans, the dismembered lion with its weird grin—everything melted into that infinite and empty desert. Even me." Omar stretched his arm out high above both of them and spread his fingers.

"I can never understand you," she said. Omar brushed her cheekbone. She put her head down, hid her eyes against his body. Her hand slowly traveled from her chin, where it had clutched the sheet, to his penis. She gripped him. "Do you hate me?"

"No."

She kissed his chest, letting her lips linger for a moment against his skin. "We're good for each other, aren't we? Aren't we?"

Her skin was soft, the desert locked in the wild strands of her hair. "Yes," he said. Her eyes were red. "We're meant for each other, Honey."

The Discovery Channel

He likes Tchaikovsky so much—as the camera lopes beside the pride—that he bites his lip. Ahead: wildebeest, tails switching the air.

The violins go shrill as lions corral a single wildebeest. Harps flock above, reeling like tireless birds, and one lion leaps across the space. The cat pedals its hind legs in that sudden lurching, and for a moment it seems like fervent interspecies sex. Yet he thinks of the glistening skull left on the African grassland; he wants to retrieve it for his collection of skulls and bones, shells and fish jaws.

He fingers the remote.

The lion bites deeply into the wildebeest's spine and the dark crumpling is like stiff paper. The lions languorously tighten their circle until each, a sigh of confident weight, drops to mouth the warm flesh. With eyes half-closed, mewling, their slow tongues lap deeply into the wounds.

The music stops; a black frame circles and consumes them. Suddenly, with bassoons burping into the air, the scene changes to lions playing and lolling against each other beneath a single tree umbrellaed upon a parched veldt.

"Languorous," it suddenly dawns upon him, means "slow, with undulations, and the inevitable involvement of the tongue."

The Rabbit War

Exactly one year after the death of her husband, Xmucane Henderson began the war of the rabbits.

As everyone had expected, Ish—as she was called—went into a black depression after the funeral. She had been left alone, except for a terrible son who had abandoned her so long ago—with never a word to follow—that she sometimes, for an instant, forgot his name.

The neighbors watched out for her well enough. After all, she was kind, even to those who bad-mouthed her because she habitually fetched from the county woods the most intricate ferns to grow in her garden beneath the northwest eaves. She was a master of green—only ferns: wet and low-lying, musty with soil... these were the things she rightfully tended. So when the earth came thudding down upon the casket of Charles Henderson, it was as if the concussion had been against her heart. And for two months, Xmucane withdrew behind the shades of her house and forbade light to come prickling its way through her mourning.

The women acknowledged her sorrow. All of them had sons and daughters, grandchildren and pets, and even husbands. But when they saw the ferns shrinking away, curling inward the way they imagined Ish surely must be doing behind the solemn walls of the darkened home, they called at her door. They brought coconut cookies and manzanilla tea. They knocked and knocked with a sense of purpose.

"Summer's around the corner," they said, "and fall close behind. Your ferns have given up on you."

"¡Dios!" Ish said, the fingers of her left hand gathered at her mouth so that she looked like a hamster remembering, suddenly, a promise.

"This won't do! You simply cannot go about hiding inside for the entire summer and then mold away during the fall. You must come out and tend to your garden."

"This just won't do," another woman said.

And that was that. Xmucane pulled up the shades, threw open the blinds, and let the sunlight come like a monsoon through her house.

The women ate their cookies and drank their tea. And it was Miss Cordon, the youngest and most eager of the ladies, who said that Ish should try her hand at roses. She should get away from those lowly ferns. All the ladies agreed. It would change her perspective, they said. Raise her spirits from the dirt, so to speak. The afternoon passed pleasantly enough and then the ladies left, ennobled by their good deed.

Xmucane looked up to heaven and said, "Chuck, forgive me, *pero* my ferns..."

She reared them back to health and ventured out to the woods for new plants. The season for morels had come and gone: Xmucane once more relegated Death to that realm too abstract and distant for everyday concerns.

All autumn and winter, Xmucane tried the women's bridge gatherings. She felt uncomfortable. She pretended to enjoy the club meetings, the teas, and even made cookies and had the women come by her home. But the good ladies of Clowerston spoke of their husbands and children. They spoke of the uncivilized nature of men, of the duty of women. Then, when they saw Ish's discomfort, they advised her to get a pet: a poodle or long-haired cat. Something fluffy.

She began the roses the following spring. She would surprise her husband, she thought, growing roses like the club ladies. She planted tiny bushes to raise them from babies, planting five on that dark anniversary of the death of her husband.

And thus began the rabbit war.

When the first buds plumped on the branches like small hearts, she felt the same wonder she had felt long ago on seeing the Morrison Hotel rise up in Clowerston: On that distant night, she had barely slept; she dreamed fitfully of pearl necklaces.

In the morning, every soft rosebud had been snipped. They were left broken on the ground.

When the next set of buds lay wilting on the ground, she awoke early and watched drab rabbits descend into her yard. They inspected each of her rosebushes first, then turned to graze the clover. Xmucane opened the front door and clapped her hands to frighten them. The rabbits moved only far enough to spy from a safe distance.

Xmucane then went into her cluttered garage and cut fencing from a large spool of chicken wire that Charles had hoarded away some twenty years before. Still, the rabbits snipped the buds that appeared over the next few days. They didn't eat them, or carry them off, but just stood on their hind legs to reach and snip each one. Xmucane made the fence higher.

In the next round, the rabbits worked together to fold down the wire and scissor the buds with their teeth. Xmucane rebuilt the fences with wood braces. The smallest rabbits, barely able to leave the warren, were sent wiggling through the seams of the fence. Xmucane resolved to completely surround the bushes with boards.

From her window, she could sip coffee or wash dishes and look out over her five wood huts. The ladies of Clowerston patiently asked what the purpose was in having roses if they were going to be covered up like trash heaps in some country person's yard.

The ladies sent Ish to the hardware store for traps.

Bob Slater brought out his wares. "This one," he said, "collapses their bodies."

Xmucane's hands went to her face.

He placed a large metal cage on the table. "See this little lever?" he said. "When the little rascals trip this baby, these spokes come down. See how they're hidden there? Ain't no way anything's living after that." He brought out another trap, larger than the others. "This is the deluxe model. Top of the line." Bob Slater could not keep a proud chuckle from bubbling out. "The rabbit goes in, trips it, and this edge here opens the critter up. Heck, Ish, it pretty near dresses it out for you. With one of these, you could live off the land forever. No more Krogers. And it's good for all kinds of animals, big or small."

Without a word, Xmucane turned around and left.

On the way home, she stopped at Barton's Pet Store and found herself staring into the face of a miniature poodle. The dog had been manicured. A pink bow set off its steel-gray curls. In the next cage, a mutt lay with its legs spread before and behind, head flat against the floor. The dog's eyebrows moved expressively as Xmucane looked at it.

"A woman like you needs a poodle," Mr. Barton said behind her. "It's a dog with class."

But Xmucane understood those eyebrows flinching above the sad eyes. "Nothing today, *gracias.*"

All week, she watched the rabbits snip the buds from her roses. As soon as one puckered heart appeared, the rabbits took it down. She boarded up the plants again and ignored the snickers of the women.

Then a curious thing happened.

Xmucane received a letter from the government saying that her son, Master Sergeant Robert T. Henderson, was dead. She read and reread the letter. She barely understood that now she was truly alone. The letter mentioned her son's wife and children, who had claimed the remains. He was buried with full military honors, the letter stated. Curiously, she felt no sadness at the news, only an odd flutter through her limbs that she could not identify. It disappeared quickly.

She realized that her son probably had told his wife and children that his parents were dead. He had wanted his world and theirs to be forever apart. He would have been angry, perhaps, at the government for sending the notice. Suddenly, Xmucane missed her husband more than ever. She longed to look into his worn face and call him Chuck. She longed to fluff a pillow for him in front of the television, kiss him on his old gray head, and tell him that she would be in the garden tending to the ferns. She longed to hear his rusty voice follow behind her: "Never mind about me, Ish. You just see to your garden."

Right away, she called Bob Slater and asked if there were traps that didn't kill. There was a long pause.

"Hell, I guess," he answered. "People make the darndest things." He said he'd have to order something like that.

"You can do it, please," she said. "I want one to hold them. I don't want to hurt them. I never want to hurt them."

But Xmucane felt that maybe she had lived her life wrong. How could it be that an old woman would not know her son? How had things changed so that she could pass through so many years and look up from her ferns and see that she was without a husband, without a son, living in a city she hardly recognized anymore, making herself for others and fighting rabbits to save red roses? She could not even remember many things about her son. He had been a quiet and gentle boy, with beagle eyes. Then, one day, he was simply gone.

When her traps finally arrived, Xmucane rushed out to buy them. She learned to cover them with clover and to put lettuce on the triggers. Back home, she removed the boards from around the bushes and placed the traps. The following morning, Xmucane walked deep into the Monroe woods. She apologized to the rabbit, then let the animal go. It sat a few feet from her, its nose moving wildly. Xmucane stamped her foot.

When she returned home, the buds lay like scattered confetti around the bushes.

The next morning, a baby rabbit strangled itself trying to squeeze out of the mesh cage. Xmucane could barely breathe as she threw a blanket over it and took it all to the hardware store. There, she placed the entire bundle on the counter and left it all—blanket, cage and rabbit—for Bob Slater to dispose of.

On the way home, she stopped for the sad dog that lay by the poodle like a carelessly handled sack. When the dog stood up, dazed and bewildered, its belly sagged. Xmucane named him Rover because it was the only dog name she knew.

"You scare away those rabbits," she said in the car. The dog's brown eyes stared up.

For three days, Rover watched the rabbits come and go every morning. His head lay peacefully between his outstretched legs and his belly lay flat against the cool ground.

Xmucane stood over the dog. "How you want me to grow roses when you just watching the rabbits? There's no taking it easy here, kiddo. You chase the animals or you go back! This is no welfare for you, you know. You hear me?"

When Rover didn't seem to understand, she reached for the collar and pulled him to the roses. "Be a dog!" she said.

Later that day, she heard Rover howling through the ravines behind her home. She could hear him crashing through the brush. She then began to imagine rabbits scampering for their lives. She imagined Rover dropping a mangled body onto her stoop, ashamed of his terrible duty to her, his lips cruel with blood.

"Ay Dios," she said, "what I am doing?"

She felt the heat of nausea and the air vanishing from her lungs. She threw herself onto her bed like a feverish woman. Her mind could not escape her haranguing of the dog, her careless demands. She had never intended for Rover to kill, only to frighten the rabbits away. She did not want torn bodies; she did not want anything like that, nothing bad at all.

Rover did not return for several days. When he came back, whimpering and scratching at the front door, Xmucane almost refused to open it. Her mind had already conjured something awful, but what she found was even more horrible: A hole in Rover's hind leg writhed with maggots. Flies and ants flickered over the moving white flesh. Xmucane screamed.

She called the vet, pleaded for him to come because she could not touch the dog. Later, she heard the terrible verdict. The dog had been shot or it had snagged its leg in wire. A serious infection set in; blood-flow was cut. Even with an amputation the infection might not be stopped. The dog would have to be put to sleep. Xmucane looked into Rover's eyes as he was carried away. The eyebrows seemed to question, but then they settled into some grim resignation, aloof and quiet.

Alone, Xmucane could not clear the image of Rover's leg. She could not remove the blank stare of the strangled rabbit. Broken bodies haunted her. The marble eyes of dead rabbits became bolts on her husband's coffin. The writhing maggots became white curtains fluttering in nocturnal winds. Afloat in that sea of death, Xmucane looked up to heaven.

"Where'd I do wrong?" she asked. "Chuck, oh, Chuck..."

Sitting at the window, wondering where her life had turned, she envisioned her son's death. She saw him running headlong through a jungle, the enemy firing close behind, his troops ambushed. She saw Bob running to escape, losing his breath, fighting to keep the branches from raking across his face, running though he knew he would die, and there was nothing left but to crash desperately through to some unnameable end. In her vision, he knew that he would die. She heard him call out to her, finally, from the other side of the world, the sweat running down into his eyes. *"Mamá, por favor, Mamá!"*

Xmucane moaned loudly at the window. Her heart knotted inside her chest so tightly that she could taste blood in her mouth. *"¡Ay Dios!"* she said. She thumped her chest; she pounded her fist over her heart to keep the awful pain of sadness from killing her. *"¡Ay Dios!"* she said again.

She rushed outside to breathe. She pounded her fists against her chest. Her mouth opened upward to the sky. She fell to her knees by a rosebush and suddenly knew that if she only destroyed the bushes she'd destroy the thing crushing her.

Xmucane kicked at the bush until it sagged. She ran to the garage for a hoe, then hacked until each bush fell, its roots upturned and clotted with dirt. Immediately, she hurried to weed her neglected ferns. She crawled on all fours, her dress turning black, her fingernails filling with dirt, and, slowly, slowly, the horrible fear in her chest melted away.

She understood then that she would have to live her life without ever asking where or how she had done things wrong. She would grow only ferns. She would go into the woods and hunt among the dank mosses to find those ferns she would nurture in the dark garden behind her home. She would grow nothing new, nor change her life in any way.

So that, when the pain and visions had ceased, when her dress and face were dirty and smudged from the moist soil, when the fingers of death were as distant from her heart as the roses from rooting, she walked to the front and said "rabbits" in a quiet voice. But somehow the word got tangled in her mouth and the sounds came burbling from her moist throat as a simple bubble that popped on her chin.

GOD'S POLYP

1) I am the narrator. I have no arms or legs. Yet I beget.

2) The universe is expanding.

3) If neutrinos have mass, we are all fucked.

4) Can you say "no arms and no legs?"

5) Say, what really is out there between the galaxies? Why is there is no even distribution of matter over space? Shouldn't an explosion in vacuity of equal force in all directions produce a homogenous array?

6) I am 47-years old. Old. Tired or angry. Who can know?

7) Knowledge or knowing is a matrix of the perceiver-complex + medium-complex + object-complex. This is the triad that in composition is called voice + purpose (medium) + audience. There is no evaluation or valuation outside of the triad: The perceiver's physiological characteristics limit the possible apprehensions (ergo-the primacy of the eye in humans—what laws would have emerged had we vision like flys?); the medium's characteristics also determine the domain of apprehension (we shall recall tidbits of quantum mechanics so popular today); and, of course, the object has characteristics which limit, constrain, define the "possible worlds" of its...

8) But life is another thing altogether.

9) Persistence of the gene, pool and individual.

10) Human social structures and politics all have their evolution. All are systems, which is to say, they fight to preserve themselves, to strengthen, to withstand the changes in environment, to fill every niche, to multiply. God, to perpetuate.

11) How like a solar system is Bohr's atom. How like a body, fleshy and maturing, the laws of nature.

12) What was it that we were talking about?

13) "One must then take refuge to an even higher degree than before in symbolic analogies" (N. Bohr to M. Born, Letter dated 1 May 1925).

14) If there is a duplication in "form," this in itself warrants belief. This is to say, in apprehending certain characteristics of an object—any object—we automatically begin the process of assimilation and of determining truth or knowledge-base regarding the particular apprehended phenomenon. There are six systems by which we humans determine such a thing, one being the system of analogies: If there exist in the world other analogous characteristics and patterns, ("allegories" in literature) no matter how far afield, then there is justification in having what we call a "belief" about the subject. Naturally, the more analogous structures there are in the world, the more compelling is our belief. Why, for instance, is Pythagorias's theorem and its measurements so alchemical if not for this most fundamental system of belief?

15) The essay is discursive, art is representational. Dictator versus contractual agreement. Today the "I" essay is at its height, when the subjectivity of the world is too overwhelming for the average cow. Where are the bulls?

16) Nothing new under the Black Holes, the neutron stars, if you will.

17) All knowledge and the imparting of knowledge is "cartographic." The interesting thing about maps is that while they perforce explicate, define, teach, reveal, represent, they necessarily lie. Nice paradox. An observer would be just as lost

in the map as s/he is in reality if the map gave every scrap and branch, every height and width, every hair and brick in a true representation of reality—if it replicated so as to be faithful. Maps can only be so good, then they are bad.

18) Imagine: I get in my car to drive from Indiana to Washington because I get this job and I reach in the glove compartment because I want a map because I don't know how to get there and anyway how the hell do I know where this rinky-dink Western Washington University is? The best map in the world he told me he'd get me. And it's a fucking surveyor's map. It shows where every bank on the Wabash is where every piece of that kind of white plastic tubing is so that water and sewage can get from one house to the other to the road and out to the sea the sea for God's sake. And the map is like something out of Borges because I open the cover and the map has so much detail that the book swells up and fills up the car and breaks my windows and almost suffocates me like an air bag by smashing me against the seat with the billions and billions of pages of information facts truths swelling out of the fine vellum and I scream Whoa humanity!—too much fucking knowledge!

19) I mean doesn't he know who I am and what I already know and how much I need to know to just have my needs met? I mean purpose is part of this triad stuff, isn't it?

20) The six systems that interplay and through which we are said to "know" something are: a) Conventionalized Factuality; b) Conventionalized Observation; c) Triadic Principle; d) Allegorical Verification; e) Definitional Truths; and f) Probabilistic Certainty. That is (follow the small letters, now: I know you can, if you try, if you aren't linked to the identification aesthetic as to a ball and chain).

21) Authority tells us what to believe. The average person knows nothing of the world except by being told and told with authority, brandished yardstick in hand. What real history do any of us know except through authority?

22) S. T. Coleridge attacked Laplacian mechanics for its "despotism of the eye" (circa look it up yourself). Just think how many people believe the marking off of hours as anything but arbitrary, believe in some basic grammar of inches, or swear by something called natural mathematics? Where the God-damn did we ever come up with metrics as anything truer?

23) Complementarity! Bow down, ye of little faith, ye who despise a cast of dice!

24) The beauty of truth is that it reverberates like art. The visions of *the* artist are echoed not only throughout but out through the world so that the work is necessary, confirming...the real world both its offspring and its parent. Both defer to the other so that beauty is truth and—how do you say in English?—vice versa. Anyway, this has already been discussed in 14).

25) $x = x$. $b = b$, the simplicity is—how do you say in physics-enese?—"beautiful," "symmetrical."

26) What keeps us moral is the very high probability that tomorrow will come. Morality is social custom.

27) Oh, Pancho, Joy, it is stupefying the number of things working at the same time, most hidden from sight or so basic that we cannot notice them. How sad that we forsake each other, how sad that time and place were positioned so inaptly, so, so...

28) "It is meaningless to talk of the position of a particle of fixed velocity. But if one accepts a less accurate position and velocity, that does indeed have meaning. So one understands very well that it is macroscopically meaningful to speak more approximately of the position and velocity of a body" (Heisenberg to Pauli, Letter dated 28 Oct. 1926).

29) How like an analogy an analogy is, how like a trope a trope.

30) Meanwhile, while pursuing the first billionths of a second after the First Explosion, physicists have cognizance of energy levels high enough to allow for parameters in equa-

tions such that symmetry exists—mathematically speaking—among three of the four forces. They say that they need to merely look out far enough in the distance so as to see the past. To unify all the forces. Supersymmetry. Snap a rubber band to that!

31) Bohr's model of the atom seems to imply stable planes or orbits for electrons when in reality one can only speak of *tendencies* or major patterns of electrons around a nucleus and not absolute orbits.

32) However, this map gets the job done. Are we back to the triad?

33) See Cassandra Mateo's "A Technique of Tropes as a Means to Understanding Magic-Realism" *(Studies on Modern and Classic Literatures and Languages;* Feb. something) for a discussion and analogy on the relationship between physics and literature. See also her "General Commentary on Readings for Folklore and Myth" (ms; n.d.) for a discussion of the non-rational or a-rational necessities of myth, suitable for beginning readers in the field and those nincompoops who insist on using "myth" to mean falsehood. See also her "Lectures on Techniques of the A-Real in Literature" (delivered at Western Washington U.) for a fascinating and compelling discussion of the "cartographic" nature of knowledge and of the painfully difficult and complex issue of varieties of unreliable narrators. Here we see the skin of telling as the ego defleshed, boned to the lie. Satan's evil is overdeveloped self-awareness.

34) Whither shall we go? From whence have we come?

35) Doubtless, the probability of finding life on other planets is high, not unlike the probability of finding minor damaged genes within an otherwise healthy body. The billions upon billions—infinite shall we say?—of subatomic particles of chromosomes, acids, proteins in a human body are not all healthy. Some are dying, some have glitches, some healthy as horses tugging spiritedly against the reins. God, their loins are so obvious, so real, so true!

36) Within the dumb and fundamental movements of the sea, there arose the bawdiness of life.

37) Gaia.

38) Only intelligent life can accelerate the natural rhythms of growth, can beget materials that beget more things in virulent numbers. Only intelligence and viruses change the genetic makeup of life around it.

39) Given sufficiently large periods of time, the planets themselves escape their orbits, wobble on their spurious legs, buckle quietly into bed.

40) In the bowels of the earth we are burying cans of radioactive material with half-lives the span of Earth itself. And the United States created a group of thinkers to think of ways to communicate with our children millions of years down the line. The problems are interesting, to be sure. They involve notions of language typology and historical linguistics, of the evolution of language, of the perceiver-complex, of story-telling. They strike at the very heart of communication, that mapping of knowledge. All this to make a sign on these poisonous canisters that we beget. All this for a sign to our children's children's children's children: "Warning: this stuff is bad for your health. Do not open until Christ."

41) The universe is finite and infinite. A closed infinite space. A body infinitely large. Remember the balloon with dots to represent stars, the raisins in dough: equidistant, equi-expansion, curved space, microscopically positionless as a thing of fixed velocity, yet macroscopically corpulent? Heat-death? Cold-death?

42) Intelligent life is the polyp growing cancerous in the universe.

43) The accelerated accumulation of matter to astronomic levels is basically what constitutes a Neutron Star—Black Hole. Black Holes eat the surrounding space. Black Holes kill. Black Holes multiply their Black Hole-ness by increasing the death of space and matter around it.

44) Thank God the Milky Way is at the extreme end of the universe. Thank God: our solar system is after the colon of this extremity.

45) See Cassandra Mateo's *Remembering to Say Mouth or Face* (I don't have arms or legs!) for a discussion of these issues and the relationship between intelligence and non-biodegradable waste material; intelligence and viruses; fiction and decadence; analysis and anuses.

46) Perhaps roughage is the answer.

High on the Precipice

Alpírez stood back and howled. Quetzil lay on his stomach, arms behind his back, legs tied to his forearms through
an ingenious armature of knots and thin, stripped sticks. The
cording looped upward, pluming at the frayed ends like corn
silk. The elaborate harness creaked when Quetzil moved and
it tightened a flat piece of board into his mouth. On the
precipice, Alpírez did a gleeful jig.

Above us, the sky? Nothing... A rumpled gray blanket,
low, *molestando*. Not even one or two birds. There was, but
away from us, as if in another world, a burping of yellow light
from great altitudes of storm and thunder. But for us, not
even the *canto de un grillo*. The wind moved across my face so
that my breath felt outside my lungs. As if speaking were not
speaking, not forcing words out, but an opening of the mouth
so that the coursing wind pulled language from my mouth.
Not speaking, not forming words. *Palabras arrancadas*.

Me puse cerca to peer down the *barranco* at the ocean
below. The grass peeled back from the rock near the peak of
the escarpment, where Alpírez and Quetzil had begun, and
the gray rock *cambio* colors only because of lichen and smat-
tered gull shit. A thick *madrona* lay bare: red bark peeled

back, like a lanced penis below vision serpents. *Dios. Era algo de los templos.* The knots and ridges of that bole were sleek; the musculature pronounced. *De los templos.*

So I yelled, "Xquic!"

Alpírez glanced at me and snarled.

He was *ladino.* I am *ladino.*

Deciding, or my body *estaba* deciding, working as it was through the anguish of *no sé qué.* Because... because *lo que siento no tiene palabras, solo imágenes de verguënza.*

I heard the thud of boot to flesh, and then the board clicking in Quetzil's mouth.

"Stop," I said. Arrancada.

Alpírez laughed. His gold epaulettes caught light.

"I mean it," I said.

Deliberately, he reached down—*OJOS*—eyes holding me, and yanked my brother's head back.

"Cabrón," I said, *"¡Cerote!"* Blood trickled from Quetzil's mouth.

Alpírez blew me a kiss and thundered a fist into my brother's kidneys; his body churned.

I looked out over the water, blue-green and chipping in the strong wind. The sea brought me the oddest scent of coffee, brewed black, toughened by salt. I heard another fist or boot thudding.

Verde, verde, verde. I tried to recall the famous lines. Tecun Uman, Tecun Uman, Tecun Uman. Tecun of the Asturian drum, drumming, drumming.

But what came back is this throb at the temple of anger.

I was not his target, so *me quedé quieto.* Why speak, when silence can make the vane point away, the forget-me-nots only beautiful flowers? *Me quedé quieto.* I looked out until the terrible sounds of my brother's pain evaporated. Lifted away *hasta...*

Imagine: a dancer *como un* weeping willow tree, slow undulations on the hilltop, arms, legs... *¡Qué maravilla!* A woman's body can show such freedom as makes a wise man humble, a petty man desirous. Arms akimbo, svelte turns, pirouettes. An ankle kicking up!

My brother shrieked. Muffled by the board. I jerked to see Alpírez peeling back like red bark the skin off my brother's back. The wide knife-blade muddied with blood.

OJOS.

I couldn't bear to watch.

I couldn't bear to watch.

I couldn't bear to watch.

I watched Alpírez click his teeth onto a blade of grass. I would not look at Quetzil. Above the water, far out, gulls now keened, cormorants now dove. Wind rushed across the crags. Farther out, farther out, nearly lost in the gray overcast, volcanoes loomed. How pretty they are with cirrus clouds passing by, nuzzling by. How pretty as they part around the volcano peak.

I should have told him to stop.

Quetzil was still alive, thank God. He struggled and made sickening groans. Another heavy thud of sole against flesh. And another.

Gulls cackled by the bluff—thank God!

Some wing flapping?

A flag of cloth, herky-jerky in the wind?

A heavy branch nodding under el cielo respirando?

No.

The woman atop the hill,
dancing...

How could Alpírez do it? Wasn't he repulsed?

I have to fight to keep from vomiting.

How can he continue?

I want to know!

¿Cómo? tell me, *pueden, cara a cara,* follow the green sleeve ordering such horrors? How can a man strip another naked, crack his face with a rifle butt—hear the breaking

bone, the ripping? What does one dream of at night, knowing a man hung from the beams by his testicles.

Until they rip off.

She dances with such abandon.

Where are the birds?

Oh,

I want to be there. With her.

Not to touch her, not, perhaps, even to speak with her.

BUT TO WATCH.

To be consumed by her abandon, her freedom, her unconscious movements. The life!

Fly buzz of Quetzil's cries. The far dance. The far dance.

The cry!

The swirl of her skirt. **Her movements. Her arms**:

Pinwheels del olvido

I. INTO PEARLS

The Song of Ishkik

From her bed, the maiden Ishkik saw only an evil sky. Tormented by blood-red flashes and screaming winds, the sky smelled like rotten eggs. She often wondered how she came to be in this land of Shibalbá. Perhaps there had been an error at her birth, perhaps she wasn't really the daughter of Blood Chief and Cadaver. Her dreams were filled with the beating of wings, the soft billowing and cooing of pigeons, the scent of mangoes ripening under a bright sun. What was up with that? Yet all this was before the sun and moon had been created; so, when she awoke she did not know what it could mean to dream of things not yet invented.

In her world, the Lords of Death clattered about like strung bones. They and the people of Shibalbá seemed to enjoy the countryside of rotting trash, poisoned rivers and puce lightning. They were ecstatic about the stench, and whirled crazily throughout the village, rattling and croaking, burping and farting, with not even one care about the clamor they raised. She wished that someday there would be a way out, and that someone would come to cast light into this dismal world.

In her dreams, she heard among the flutter of wings a soft voice saying words she could not quite make out. Every night, just as she felt ready to catch the words, a song interrupted:

Oh, Cacao Woman, Oh, Rain Woman,
Come and nourish here, come and agree.
Oh, Ripeness and Brightening,
Whisper sweetly to me.

For three nights she heard the song, always as she nearly, almost caught the whispering. Then on the fourth night, the song did not come and the voice spoke to her.

"There is a gourd tree," it said in a whisper like the beating of hummingbird wings. "Go and find it at Dusty Court. Go and you will see the fruit it bears."

When she awoke, she went to her father at the ball court where he and the other Lords of Death watched a gruesome game. They threw garbage at the players, insulted them and even threw their own bones and arms to trip them up. They sacrificed everyone.

"I have heard of a gourd tree," she said to her father.

The blood ran from his eyes and pooled at his feet. His hair bristled. "No one is to go near Gourd Tree," he bellowed.

The other Lords stopped and listened. One Death and Seven Death, the leaders of Shibalbá, raised their scepters. "It is our decree that no one shall go near this tree," they both said. "It is an evil among us. It bears fruit. Its leaves are green and full. It's too pretty!"

"It is horrible," added Wound Master in his sharp voice.

All the Lords then gathered around her: Bone Staff, Skull Staff, Filth Master, Pus Maker, Bile Maker, Flying Noose, Talon and Hawk. "It is our decree!" they all shouted at her so that her ears hurt.

She ran down the steps of the ball court, onto the dirt road, down along the shore of Blood River and into Woods of Dead and Dying Trees. She ran and ran until she suddenly found herself within Dusty Court. There, before her, rose the wonderful Gourd Tree. Its trunk loomed high. The branches, muscled and blue-green, sprouted thick bouquets of leaves. It turned the wretched Shibalbá into a lush green she could not have imagined for herself no matter how many times she dreamed of life, of beauty, or of what rises from ashes.

Within that deep greening, round gourds gleamed white.

"What if I were to cut just one?" she said to herself. "They look so delicious, so fat with seeds."

Then a fruit spoke to her. "What do you want with skulls made to look like fruit?"

Ishkik started. Then she saw clearly that one of the gourds was not a gourd at all, but a skull that looked tired and sad from hanging so long. Had it earlobes, they would have drooped.

"Go away," it said. "You don't want this fruit."

"But I do! I do want the fruit growing secretly here."

"Then stick your right hand out. Come nearer."

Ishkik moved closer and smelled the richness of the bearing tree. When she stretched her right hand out, the skull spit into her hand. The spit became a seed in her palm and then it disappeared altogether.

"People take fright of bones," the skull said. "But remember, one's children are like seeds which grow the fruit again. Whether it is the child of a king or the child of a beggar, life is not lost. It goes on for those not trapped in death. For the image of a lord or warrior, or for the image of a sage or individual, there will remain the daughters, the sons. Go now. Rise up to earth, for you shall enter into the word. You will not die. You will be a carrier of peace. Let your voice rise against hateful things."

Ishkik returned home and felt the changes taking place within her. She was filled with joy. The secret voice inside her sang:

> Oh, Cacao Woman, Oh, Rain Woman,
> Come and nourish here, come and agree.
> Oh, Ripeness and Brightening,
> Whisper sweetly to me.

In four months, her father saw that she was pregnant.
"How can this be?"
"Father," she said, "I have not known any man!"
Yet Blood Chief called all the Lords of Death to council and told them of the evil of his daughter.
"She is to be done away with," the Lords proclaimed. "Send for our messengers and have them sacrifice her!"
The four owls came: one was Parrot Owl, with his scorched colors; one was Skull Owl, with his ravaged body; one was Knife Owl with scars and twisted quills; the last was One Leg Owl. They came with White Knife to sacrifice the maiden Ishkik.
"Take her away and bring her heart back to us!" the Lords said.
Ishkik floated between the owls, carried away by their rapidly beating wings.
"Oh, Owls," she pleaded, "it can't be that you will kill me. I am like you. I have been mistreated. This is not our place." With tears flowing from her eyes, she sang:

> Oh, Cacao Woman, Oh, Rain Woman,
> Come and nourish here, come and agree.
> Oh, Ripeness and Brightening,
> Whisper sweetly to me.

The owls were moved by her singing and they saw the truth of her words. They knew she was right: each of them had learned the cruelty of their Lords, those who only saw how to hurt and punish others.

"Very well," they said. "But what shall we do? What shall we take back to them?"

"We need a substitute heart," she said.

"The sap of the croton tree," Skull Owl said, "is the blood and heart of the tree."

Ishkik cried out to them again. "Oh, take that, please!"

Knife owl circled and—*thwunk*—he opened the bark of the croton. The dark sap ran red into the jar held out by Parrot Owl.

This will be your imitation heart," One Leg Owl said. "What they will receive will be only what their foul minds have created. What they want to see is death so that is what they will find."

The Owls took her to Earth-Road, above the cavernous world of Shibalbá.

"You will be loved on earth," she said to the owls. "You will be a sign for those who understand the good that runs through life."

"And you will find your true place in the brightness of light," the owls replied.

The owls then returned with the false heart. The Lords circled around a great fire, a stinking fire, with flames licking into the sulfurous, gray air. And there, the Lords pitched in the sap of the croton. A dark incense swirled among the Lords, who cackled and danced over destroying a maiden's heart, for it is only evil that begets evil and peace that begets peace.

Far above them, where the green hills roll and the waters of the earth flow like crystal, Ishkik gave birth to twins. She lay beneath the sweet shade of Yax tree and named them Blowgunner and Jaguar Sun, in honor of the sun and moon which were yet to come as part of the vision of the Lords of Heaven. It would be they who lit up the sky and brought light to the world. Ishkik rocked her swaddled boys and listened to the Muan Bird singing in the branches above. The bird sang:

Oh, Cacao Woman, Oh, Rain Woman,
Come and nourish here, come and agree.
Oh, Ripeness and Brightening,
Whisper sweetly to me,
Of what is near and coming
For this Earth, so muddled,
so dear.

Let those of darkness
and those of daylight
find strength in bright words,
nourishing words, within
the peaceful worlds
strong words bring into view.

The Grackle

It made little difference to Gertie Danse whether she worked late at night or early in the morning, so long as one did not follow the other too quickly. By day, the sun warmed her fingers as she carved soapstone, but she heard the thrashing of nearby tractors. Living just outside Clowerston, she found the quietness of night pleasant. She believed more in her sense of touch then, in her feel for the curve of a candleholder. Yet the night air made her kneecaps ache. It was a matter of trading niceties, and of living with maladies.

One day, after speaking at length with Mr. Fletcher about a particular table piece she was fashioning for him, she cocked her head to one side and listened carefully. She heard the flapping of wings against paper. Something was surely wrong. It came from just below her eastern window. Gertie reached for her cherry cane and poked her way out the door. The flapping stopped momentarily, then came more fervently.

"Oh, no," Gertie said. "I won't hurt you. Don't you worry." She took several cautious steps and the flapping stopped. "It's a bird," Gertie exclaimed.

They waited quietly only a few feet apart.

"Come on now, birdie. Make a little noise so I can help you." She moved nearer. "Did you see sky in my window? Is that what happened?" Still there was no noise.

Gertie chirped to draw it out.

"How can I help you, if you won't help me? Come on, little one."

And then the rustling was at her feet. "Ah-hah! Don't be afraid," she whispered. "Look at you, caught in this paper. No, don't struggle. Let me feel your wings. What's all this paper doing here, anyway?"

"It's your newspaper," the bird said. "And don't press so hard."

"What!"

"Be careful, I said."

Gertie collapsed below her window. "Who's playing jokes here? Who's there? Show yourself!"

"It's just the two of us," the bird said.

"But ..."

"Yes, yes: birds don't talk! If I had a dime for every time I heard that."

Gertie was speechless.

"I'm sure you've noticed my accent."

Come to think of it, Gertie could detect an odd accent in the bird's speech. She reached for her cane, dropped in her surprise, and tried to place the accent. It was like a Maine accent, but with a toothless whistle at each "s." The "k's" were soft, as well. Gertie rubbed the length of her cane in thought.

The bird looked warily back. "You aren't going to kill me, are you?"

"Oh, no!" Gertie said.

"Well, are you going to help me or not?"

"Oh, yes!"

"Hurry, then. It hurts like hell."

"Please don't swear," Gertie said.

The bird turned its beak away and said, "Just get me inside and bandaged up. I think one of my wings is broken."

"But how ...?"

"Just get me inside, will you. I'll probably die if you don't hurry."

Gertie lifted the bird in one hand.

"Not so hard!"

With the cane in the other hand, Gertie tapped her way into the kitchen. She found a dishtowel with which to make a bed, and then set herself to examining the wings and legs.

"There doesn't seem to be anything broken," she said. "I don't feel a lump or anything."

The bird moaned. "I'm sure it's broken."

Gertie touched along the bones. Aside from making the bird a splint, there was little she could do anyway. She touched here and there, all the time asking the bird if it hurt here or there. The bird groaned and complained so much that finally Gertie gave up trying to find exactly where it hurt.

"I'm sorry," she said, "but I can't find anything."

The bird moaned loudly and fell into a swoon. "My mother..." he gasped, "used to, to... to tell us that corn—O, the pain!—corn will help!" And with that, the bird fell limp within Gertie's hand.

"Oh, my," she said. "Are you dead?"

The bird opened one eye. "No, but I don't know how long I'll hold out."

"Just wait. I'll find some corn. Wait."

"Hurry. Hurry!"

Gertie climbed a chair by the kitchen cabinets and felt each container until she found the correctly inscribed coffee can. It was empty. "I'm out of corn."

"Bread, then. And a little milk, too. Not too much."

"Gee, I hope I have milk. I should, you know." She reached for the bread in the lower cabinet. "I drink my coffee with milk. One cup in the morning. No more since it's bad for you. Coffee olé, they call it. It tastes better with milk, I think. Certainly better than with coffee creamer."

The bird moaned hideously.

Gertie put the bread by the bird and rummaged through the refrigerator. "It's amazing that you can talk. Amazing. Yes, there's milk. I've never heard anything like it." She put the milk by the bread. "I'll get you a bowl. A talking bird! Where are you from?"

"Vermont," the bird said, one wing draped over its face.

"Vermont! I've heard of that." Gertie shredded pieces of bread into the bowl, then poured milk. "Tell me when to stop."

"Stop."

"I don't know where Vermont is, though."

"Stop!"

Gertie held the milk carton against her side. "Did I pour too much?"

"For Christ's sake, it's fine!"

"I would appreciate it if you did not swear in my house." Gertie walked stiffly to the refrigerator with the milk. "I do not like people to swear. It's so unbecoming. So vulgar." She laughed suddenly. "I guess I don't like birds swearing, either."

The bird ate noisily, slurping the milk and smacking its beak as it chewed.

Gertie sat quietly beside the bird. She thought it impolite to speak while the bird ate, so she waited to ask the questions that burned to be asked. After some minutes, the bird clacked its beak with satisfaction.

"What kind of bird are you?"

"A grackle." The bird stood and stretched. He stroked the milky bread from around his face.

"What should I call you?"

"Bird."

"Just bird?"

"No. My name is Bird. Capital 'B.' "

"My name's Gertie." She smiled. "I wish we could shake hands, Bird."

"You're a clever one, aren't you?"

Gertie chuckled appreciatively.

"I think I need to rest."

"You just rest for as long as you like. My home is yours."

"Thanks, Tía."

"I'll just clean up here and then go into my workroom. If you need anything, let me know. You just rest."

"Okay."

"Don't hesitate to call, either. If you need anything. Anything."

"Okay."

"Or maybe it would be better if I didn't clean right now, but let you rest. I'll go into the workroom so you can rest. Call if you need anything, okay? Just feel free ..."

"Okay!"

Gertie waited by the wall separating it from the front room until she heard the slow snoring of Bird. It was important to make sure the little fellow felt comfortable. The poor creature could go into shock or something after smashing into the house. She wondered if she should put posters in the middle of her windows that showed trees or rivers, something that the birds would not try to fly through. But everything she thought of was something birds liked to fly *to*, so it was the same.

In the workroom, Gertie stroked the thigh of a figurine. She pursed her lips in concentration. Then, with a fine-grain sander that buzzed like a horsefly, she enhanced the dimpled knee. She gently stroked the leg after each minute rasping. She paid particular attention to the figurine's calves as a way of stalling work on the toes. She had always dreaded making toes. She felt inadequate to the delicate task, though really it was the case that she thought the human foot preposterous, silly even, or ugly. As of late, she had taken to hiding the feet of figurines beneath fronds or rumpled blankets. In her fifty years as an artisan, toes had remained her nemesis. She often thought it was her blindness that made it so. Yes, she decided again, it was the blindness that had always hindered her toe-making.

Bird called out, breaking through Gertie's concentration.

Gertie smoothed a velvet cloth on the table. She carefully folded the corners of it around the figurine.

The grackle fluttered in the living room as if annoyed by the very floor. Gertie heard Bird's gestures as well as if she had eyes. The wings raised abruptly, then swept across the room as he pointed.

"What's wrong?" Gertie said.

"Look at this! Look at all this nonsense you have cluttering the room. Figurines! Candlesticks! What exactly do you call all this?"

"I make them," Gertie said. "I make them and sell them. That's what I do."

"People actually buy this junk?"

"Don't you like them?"

"Like what? How could anyone with taste like them?"

"What's wrong?"

Bird hopped on the coffee table and walked around a soapstone chess set. "Just look at this!" He fanned the white king's face with his wing tip. "Disgusting!"

"What?"

"They're so...so, human!"

Gertie sat in her wicker chair, her hands awkward lumps on her lap.

"Are you an artist?" Bird said.

"I beg your pardon?"

"At least you don't have toes on these monstrosities."

"I can't make toes."

"Nevertheless, this," Bird said with a sweep of his wing, "is garbage!"

"These are just things I sell," Gertie said. She straightened. "Wait. Let me show you something."

She hurried to the workroom. Bird walked behind Gertie, all the time huffing and "tsk-ing" as he saw the myriad carved forms set about the house.

"Here it is," Gertie said, touching a statue.

The sculpture was of three men wrestling and grappling for a ball. The naked men were caught as they pushed each other's arms, grimaced at each other, fended off each other's attacks. The lilac-colored ball rested demurely by their entangled feet. Off to one side, a woman in a tennis outfit laughed. Her racket angled jauntily at her hip.

Bird choked back a laugh.

"What's the matter now?"

"Listen, Tía. What you have is a lack of understanding. Why, in my home country of Versant ..."

"I thought you said Vermont."

"No. Versant. You're not listening."

Bird flew and perched himself on the statue next to Gertie.

"Why," he said, "where I'm from, painters paint on mountains! Sculptors fashion tremendous eagles springing from the breasts of beagles. It's a world that understands the mysteries of life, girl! And here you are, wasting time by making simple puppets. You make mockery of the gift of life by squandering it. By making these *figurines!* These soapstone ashtrays. Why, they're *all* ashtrays!"

"Well, I don't know ..."

"That's right! You don't know. Hell!"

"Don't swear."

"You're blind through and through!"

Bird put a wing across Gertie's shoulder. His voice softened. "Look, Gertie, I don't mean to hurt your feelings. I'm only trying to help you. Open up, girl! You can't go on with this nonsense."

Gertie's shoulder's sagged. Her head bowed.

"Perk up. I'll help you."

"But how?"

"You have to trust me."

"I don't know."

"You'll have to change everything."

"Everything?" Gertie asked.

"This is your chance to break free."

"But I'm too old."

"You're never too old. Why, I bet you've always wanted to change. I bet you've always wanted to say the hell with toes! Just think: It'll be as if your toe-less life never existed. This is your last chance, maybe. Perk up! Let yourself go! Unzip the skin of your familiar self and step into the new!"

Gertie rubbed her forehead. "Gee," she said. "It's hard to change."

"That's why you need me. Think of it as good fortune. I showed up just when you needed me the most. Like an idea waiting to be entertained."

"Gee."

"'Gee,' she says."

"Okay, don't make fun of me." Gertie moved to her bench. Her hand opened the velvet cloth and stroked the legs of the figurine.

"I'm sorry, Tía. You took me in because I was sick and needy, like a fresh start, and now I can return the favor. I can help you."

Gertie's fingers found the lumps at the end of the figurine's legs. She would have to do something with them. "Okay," she said. "What do we do?"

"Explode!" shouted Bird. He flew to the worktable. "You need to explode!"

"Explode, huh?"

Bird spoke gloriously about the artists of Versant. Bird rose up on the back of a recliner and shook his wing; he flew to a window ledge and made orations against the darkness settling outside. Far into the evening, Gertie listened to the teachings of Bird. Gertie paced back and forth as Bird flew the full length of the house. Gertie turned her head this way and that way as she listened. The language became rhythmic chanting or religious urging. Gertie paced with the fervor of a new convert. She clapped her hands and let long sighs slip between her teeth. And that very night, late indeed, in a fever

pitch, Bird sent Gertie to fashion from soapstone the passionate complaints of walnuts. "Transcend!" Bird shouted with
encouragement.

They slept late the following morning.

While Bird slept, Gertie rigged a perch by the kitchen
table. The hot smells of breakfast slipped down the hall and
into the bedroom where Bird slept, prying open his eyelids
with appetite. He entered the kitchen, all bleary-eyed from
the evening's evangelism. He barely saw the perch, even
though Gertie stood by it like a beaming wife. Bird uttered a
groan of half pain and half pleasure.

They ate greedily.

Once revived, Bird gestured with his fork. "Today," he
said, "we'll tackle those toes. You're outward bound, my
friend."

Gertie smiled sheepishly.

All that day, Gertie reworked the figurine for Mr. Fletcher. Starting over, she copied everything except the toes. With
wild abandonment, she gave the "pin-up" proportionate
Woman-on-Sofa very enormous toes. They swelled up from her
feet and glistened above like useless soap bubbles. "American
Bondage," Gertie called it. Bird looked up from a bowl of cere-
al and clacked praise.

"It's too much, isn't it?"

Bird scoffed.

"I can put socks on the feet. Mr. Fletcher will never notice
what's underneath."

"If," Bird said angrily, "Mr. Fleck-shirt needs a sock of
realism to disguise Truth, he doesn't deserve the work."

Over the weeks, Gertie made huge noses with jelly jars
nestled in each nostril. She made bouquets of women's fingers.
She made soup pots with boiling sequoias and thunderheads,
sandwiches of mesas and plateaus. Working for days, she
carved a thumb back-packing inside a whale. She created a
series of sculptures honoring the evolution of apathy within
Clowerston River.

Mr. Fletcher knocked at the door one day.

Gertie was startled upon receiving him, as if awakening abruptly from ecstatic dreams.

"Come in," she said.

"Thank you, Gertie," he said. "I've come to see the work. How is it getting on?"

"I'm finished!"

"Wonderful."

Gertie asked him to sit and wait. She returned with the new figurine wrapped in velvet cloth. With much pomp, she unraveled her work.

Mr. Fletcher barely breathed. He sat quietly for so long that Gertie whispered, "Mr. Fletcher?"

"Is this a joke?" he asked.

"No."

"I don't know what to say, Miss Danse."

"Miss Danse?" Gertie asked.

"This must be a joke." Mr. Fletcher lifted a crease from his pants. "Now, I would like to see the real work."

"This is it."

Mr. Fletcher measured the toes against the stripes in Gertie's shirt. "I'm sorry, Miss Danse, but this will not do. It is not what I had asked for."

"You must realize, Mr. Fletcher, the transcendency of art."

"I realize," he answered slowly, "only that I have been misled into believing you as the artist to commission. I don't understand why people recommended you. Perhaps this an elaborate joke at my expense, perhaps you're just... forgetful."

"This is the first sale of my new art, Mr. Fletcher."

"No. You are most definitely wrong. This is not your first sale."

Gertie leaned forward and clapped her hands in Mr. Fletcher's face. "I have given up the squalor of making simple figurines," she said. "This is the last figurine I will make. No

longer will I merely mimic human bodies, but portray the pre-
occupations, the fears and joys, the secret obsessions springing like beagles from the breasts of people!"

"I have to go now, Miss Danse."

Gertie moved to block the door.

"Don't try to stop me."

"You really don't want the work?"

Mr. Fletcher placed a hand on Gertie's wrist. "May I sug-
gest you see a doctor? You're not getting any younger, you
know. Tom Sullivan is an excellent doctor, Gertie." He patted
her wrist with two fingers, then left.

"You did wonderfully!" Bird said, entering from where he
had been listening.

"He thinks I'm crazy. Old and crazy."

"A mere pedestrian!" Bird settled onto the coffee table.
"You need to break the walls of ignorance here in Clowerston.
You need to do something that will leap into the minds of
these Midwesterners."

"Gee."

Bird clicked his beak in sudden enthusiasm. "A monument so large and imposing that the most stalwart imbecile
will succumb!"

"I don't know..."

"Are you with me, Tía?"

"Gee..."

"That a girl!"

"But what do I do?"

Bird stroked his beak. He crossed and uncrossed his legs.
"I have it! A monument in the park."

"Hmm," Gertie said. "The town council has been asking
me for years to contribute a work."

"A journey of the imagination," Bird mused. "A free lift
into enlightenment. Perfect!"

Right then and there, Gertie dressed neatly so she might
walk into town.

The mayor thanked her for her generosity. The Alderman praised the foresight of the project: "Clowerston's only living artist won't be around forever," he said wisely. The Chief of Police gave Gertie an official peck on the cheek.

So, for week after week, Gertie toiled beneath a large tent in the town park. She never revealed to anyone, not even to prying reporters, what she was up to. *The Daily Herald*, consumed with unsatiated curiosity, removed the headlines chronicling the rash of dog murders and billed Gertie's monument as the greatest event in the recent history of Clowerston. As time went on, the Town Council saw the opportunity for a little public relations. It organized a fair for the unveiling so that once an out-of-town band was hired, merchants' licenses went like begonias.

On the day of the unveiling, the council lamented that it hadn't organized a parade. The day was marvelously nice.

Gertie dressed in her navy-blue suit. In place of her cherry cane, she carried a black lacquered cane. Bird said he would watch from a nearby tree. "The moment is yours," Bird said.

The band played "When the Saints Come Marching In" as thousands of balloons were released over the park. The mayor lauded old Gertie Danse and confirmed what the heart of Clowerston knew: that Ms. Danse had lived many years in the service of this great town of Clowerston, Indiana, and had served well! Amid roaring cheers, the tarpaulin was pulled away by a wench on the back of the Alderman's pickup truck.

Gertie had carved a yawning mountain with sundry writing tools spewing from the maw like crumbling teeth. Pencils and erasers, envelopes and school tablets avalanched over the mountain's chin.

The town of Clowerston was stupefied. Children laughed until their sides hurt. The adults turned to one another as if they had seen chicken bones growing from each others' noses. Only Mr. Fletcher spoke, and he spoke loudly against Gertie Danse. He pointed at her and shouted to friends, "I told you so! I told you so!" The mayor and Alderman stepped quickly to the side of the mountain and conferred nervously.

Gertie stepped slowly down from the stage and walked the long way home.

For the remainder of the afternoon, an errand boy knocked frequently at Gertie's door to notify her of canceled commissions. The last and final blow came when Miss Cordon from the library said that she would be returning the swan bookends she had donated four years earlier.

Gertie ate quietly that night. She could bring herself to make only canned hominy and baked beans. Bird refused to eat.

"They're oafs," Bird said. "Simpletons. What do they know, anyway?"

Gertie coughed.

"You must grow wings, Gertie. It's the only way to overcome this place. Tonight, I want you to stand in your bedroom window and leap out head first. It is time to grow wings! It's all or nothing, Tía!"

"I can't do that."

"You've gone too far to turn back now."

"No," Gertie said. "I've gone too far."

"No artist of Versant would say that!"

"I guess I'm no artist of Versant. Can't we compromise a little on this? Isn't there any way?"

"No!" Bird paced in front of Gertie's plate. "I trusted you, Gertie. I cared for you. I've shown you the way out, the light. You're not getting any younger, you know."

Gertie groaned and clapped her hands over her ears. "This has gone too far. Too far. Even the library is returning my swans. Everyone is upset with me. They think I'm senile."

"Hang the library! And this entire, insignificant village!"

"Maybe they're right, Bird."

"They're not right!"

"But I can't sell my work."

"Only peons sell to pedestrians."

"But I want others to like what I do."

Bird raised a fork and pointed at Gertie. "Grow wings tonight, Tía... or walk forever!"

"I can't. I just can't. We need to change things. It's gone too far."

"Change nothing!"

"We need to change things in the relationship."

"What!" Bird jabbed a wing in Gertie's face. "What do we need to change? Tell me!"

Gertie blushed away.

"Don't get cow with me! If you don't like something, you'd better tell me now."

"Well," Gertie said, "Please try to see what I need. I need to sell my work. I need people to like what I do. I can't just go off into a private world. I can't be pushy to other people. You can't be pushy to me."

"Pushy! Pushy!" Bird's fork clattered to the table.

"I mean 'aggressive.'"

"Aggressive!" Bird slapped his wings to his sides. "That does it! I've cared for you! I've tried to teach you! You're nothing but a selfish old woman! You expect people to feel sorry for you just because you're blind, don't you? You think you can take advantage of them because they don't want to hurt you. Well, I'll tell you one thing: You can't! And I thought you could learn something about art. Hah!"

"No," Gertie said. "I don't mean that."

"I stayed here because I felt sorry for you. I wanted to help you. What am I getting out of this? Huh? Nothing! Well, I don't feel sorry for you anymore. If you're going to be insulting and rude, I won't stay. I have feelings, too, you know?"

"Look, Bird..."

"I want an apology."

"Can't you see what I need?"

"You won't do it, will you? Your natural rudeness won't let you. Very well!" Bird flew to an open window. "This is your last chance. Either jump out this window with me now, or rot here with the rest of these ignoramuses!"

Gertie shredded her paper napkin.

"Fine," Bird said. "We are friends no more!"

And with that, Bird flew from the window and disappeared into the glare of street lamps.

Gertie could not completely suppress the word "wait." She flinched as if to move toward the window, but the word came so quietly that Bird could not have heard it if he'd wanted to.

Several months later, in the soothing light of morning, while she rubbed the toes of a newly carved figurine, Gertie heard a disjointed fluttering of wings. She laughed suddenly, thinking that a bird in paper is better than two inside the house. Then she realized that she had altered the saying too much. It wasn't really funny upon second thought. She tried, for several minutes, to reshape the saying in a sensible fashion. She found that she couldn't and that she couldn't for the life of her see why she had laughed in the first place. The fluttering became so loud that Gertie walked clear across the workroom and turned her radio loud.

Jazz.

Under a Blinding Sun

Only because the land had forsaken them did Isabel Quievac see her son disappearing. The drought had so caked him with dirt that she hurried outside to wipe his face and hands.

"Hunapu!" she called out, brushing past her husband as if he didn't exist and not wanting to hear another word from him about how she carried on about their only son.

Demetrio stood by as she took the large blue cloth to the boy's face. It was an old argument, and it was too hot to argue. He could barely swallow from the dryness of his throat. He watched her caresses, her mouth pursed with motherly concern. Demetrio briefly recalled their marriage night, when the heat then had been filled with moisture and promise.

Now, the earth lifted around them, to whirl away like smoke. Their cornstalks were mostly dead. Those still alive were brittle, the ears small and hard. They had been eating black and crumbly tortillas for days. Even the beans, soaked for a day longer than usual, ended up chewy and flavorless. And no amount of prayer seemed to save them from this misfortune.

So, it was with strange relief that Demetrio heard his wife scream. For a moment he thought that the boy was gone, burned out of his mother's heart by the blistering and unforgiving heat, no longer hunted by this harsh life.

But Isabel held out Hunapu's arm for her husband while she clamped the cloth to her mouth to quell what had taken shape in her throat. A small area above the boy's left elbow had disappeared. There was nothing there, no blood or flesh or pain, just an empty space that revealed the ground below, gray and lifeless.

Isabel dared not speak for fear some unknown thing might leap from her mouth. Her eyes were as wild and as full of bewilderment as a baby's.

Demetrio leaned down and put his arm around her. He tried lifting her to her feet, but the weight of horror crushed his wife down.

"It is nothing," he said. "It will be all right."

Hunapu, still a gangly and awkward boy, nodded slowly for Isabel. He twirled his finger in the space of his arm, then held the hole to his eye like a periscope.

Demetrio led Isabel into the hut, where he placed his trembling wife into the hammock. He sat with her until she closed her eyes and slept. The boy went away.

From the kitchen, Demetrio's mother glared. "That wife," she said.

"Don't wake her. It's difficult for her."

"And no wonder! The way she carries on about a son!"

Demetrio rubbed his eyes with both hands.

"Leave her," Consuela said.

"No!"

"She's no wife for my son. Does she make love like a wife should?"

"I will not have this!"

"¡Dios! She stays awake all night, not for you, but because she fears the dark will steal her son. All these years!"

"Please go," he said.

He looked down into Isabel's face, gentle in the day, undisturbed, sleeping and dreaming while others walked about. No, he knew it was not the dark orbits of planets, but the brilliant sun, hot and revealing, that stole life away.

Demetrio gathered two candles, one red the other white; a piece of *copal*; several cigars; and a small bottle of rum. He looped the long tassel of his belt around the items, then tied them all into a ball that hung at his waist. He would go visit Maximón, now that his prayers in church produced nothing. He had given the priest his chance, but it seemed beyond those blessed saints to save any of them. And sorrow is a heartworm gnawing at vulnerable flesh.

At the guardian's hut he paid one *quetzal* for the privilege of seeing the idol, Maximón. The *telenel* brought Demetrio in, then extinguished the lights except for a solitary candle. Demetrio could feel hope flutter inside his heart.

Maximón wore two felt hats, tens of scarves around his neck and uncountable layers of clothes. The brilliant colors seemed to glow under the candle. The *telenel* placed a short cigar into the hole of Maximón's mouth to finish the preparation.

Demetrio knelt down and made the sign of the cross. He came not for himself, he said, placing the candles at arm's reach between him and Maximón. He lit the wicks, red, then white. But for all of us, he said. Demetrio passed the *copal* over the flames twice, then the bottle of rum, and quickly the cigars. He offered them all at Maximón's feet. Demetrio prayed for rain to kill the drought. He prayed for just enough corn so that he and his wife could eat, for food so that his family might make it through this terrible time and live long enough to honor the *cofradía*—the brotherhood—the patron saints, and all the deities of the Tzutujil.

"Do this for me," he pleaded, "and unclasp the fear pinned inside Isabel."

The *telenel* walked with Demetrio to the street. "We are all saddened for you," he said.

"Maltioch," he answered—thanks—and walked home.

Demetrio found Isabel busily piling swatches of cloth in the middle of the room until Hunapu sat inundated, like Maximón, by shirts, pants, Demetrio's old hats and Isabel's scarves. She strung sandals around his neck like a necklace, then splashed her jewelry onto him so that he would shine as with disks of water.

"Look!" Isabel cried.

She lifted up the veil of clothes. Hunapu's knees had completely evaporated. His right shoulder was gone. Under the hats, the hair and scalp had vanished. Isabel's lips moved with her anguish. She passed her hand through the air of her son's chest.

"He's leaving us," she whimpered.

Demetrio's mother spoke. "She wants to cover him with clothes, as if the weight alone will make him live!"

"What do you know of how I feel?" screamed Isabel.

Demetrio stepped between them.

"You have your sons!"

Consuela touched Demetrio's firm arm.

Isabel stared up at him, pleading with her eyes for Demetrio to save their son. He turned from her and looked deeply into the boy's face. To Demetrio, Hunapu's eyes were those of a sailor's, distantly yearning, not for the betraying land of their small fields, but for the horizons and the sea swells.

"Does it hurt?" Demetrio asked.

"Oh, yes," Isabel said, "yes!"

And beside his mother's crying, the boy's jaw and neck slowly dissolved to become more mote-filled air.

Isabel opened her mouth, wet with sadness, and prayed loudly to whatever gods cared to hear: "Deign to come. Deign to catch the dust of earth, deign to clean what has been endangered, O, Five Destinies. Deign to come, our uncles, our priests, Seven Serpent, Urgent Flower. Deign to come and see what there is to salvage. Scour this black longing."

Her prayer came again, louder and louder as if to shut out the unhappy world and her despair.

Consuela hissed in the shadows.

"Be kind," Demetrio said.

That night he fell asleep hearing his wife's prayers. He too had prayed, but quietly, in bed, pleading for Maximón to save them.

In the morning he found his wife still awake, squeezing blood from wounds in her breasts. She tried coating the vanishing areas of her son, hoping to paint with her blood the absent limbs.

"Pray for your son," she yelled, "not for rain! Our son, Demetrio. Pray for our son!"

Only the boy's distant eyes, faint and illusory, remained above the vanishing torso. Below, only wisps of shoulder, ghosts of flesh, in that nebulous son.

"How can you be so unloving? How can you stand and watch your son disappear from our lives? How?"

"You are my wife," he said, and left.

She screamed out her hate of him. Consuela watched from the doorway.

All around, the tragedy of the drought ran like a rabid dog. Homes lost their children, their elders. The sky was forever a maelstrom of dirt and brittle plants; above, the sun burned the life from birdsong and downed the gluttonous vultures. Men refused to smile at one another even when humor, however maniacal, was all that could save them from total despair: To smile would allow the heat to steal the moisture of their mouths. Children looked thirstily at mothers, crying over dying family. It was a time of the Green Calendar, of destruction.

Demetrio went again to Maximón, but the line to pray extended down to the empty riverbed. Back in his field, Demetrio opened the veins of his prized turkey and pleaded with the sun. He pierced his tongue with the point of a knife and dripped the blood into the soil.

"Just clarity for Isabel," he said. "Clear the moon from her eyes. Just clarity," he said.

Behind him, Isabel came running with a bundle of clothes. She cursed him, holding out the cloth that cradled now only the eyes of her son. Like a cat peering from a stack of wood, the boy's eyes burned low and red.

"This is what you have done! This is what your complaining has done. You have killed your son, Demetrio Quievac! You and your mother have killed him."

Demetrio heard his mother yell out from the house: "See! Now she is blaming us! What won't she imagine?"

"Witch!" Isabel yelled back.

Demetrio pulled his wife by the arm. He led her across the barren field, through the ruined corn and to the dry riverbed where stones crowded the land. He pushed her hand down onto them and drew it harshly back up to her face, her fingers smeared with old dust.

"We are dying!" he said. "We won't live if this continues. Don't you see?"

"I see my son vanishing. I see you and your mother turned against me."

"No! See there!" He pointed to the gnarled trees collapsing on the banks of the dead river like old men, their roots shriveled and gray like the carcasses of iguanas. This sun is killing us. It is destroying us!"

"But my son, Demetrio..." Isabel's voice weakened and fell as she collapsed to the ground.

"I love you," he said. "We can do nothing when the gods choose for us." He held his hand out. "You are my wife, Isabel."

The eyes of the boy seemed to flicker like candlelight in the wind.

"If we don't face this drought, we'll die, Isabel. We must do something. It will not go away simply because we don't face it."

She looked up at her husband. "I'm so afraid, Demetrio."

He sank beside her and rocked her within the folds of his arms. He kissed her face, her eyebrows, the softness of her mouth, her chin. "I love you," he said. "You."

She watched the boy's eyes quietly die there beside them. Then Isabel's heart lurched, again desperate for her son. His eyes flickered like embers in the hearth of her desire.

"Let him go," Demetrio whispered, his breath filling her ear, filling the emptiness of heart there in that barren land. "Let him go."

And the eyes winked out.

The Odd Time of Raúl Sombra

There was nothing whatsoever strange, no indication that the day would be unique. In fact, it took some time for Raúl Sombra to notice that everyone else in the world had stopped moving. Only after hearing—for the first time—the sound of his own footfalls rasping down the sooty street, did he straighten and look about to see that, indeed, no one moved around him.

His shoulders sagged and he set his violin case down. He walked cautiously to a couple, caught crossing the street as they walked from store to store—perhaps shopping for rings since the handsome man held his chin high and the woman looked coyly across her companion's deep chest. He walked up to them, taking care to bow low for the woman and not presume to look into her eyes, and he apologized for halting them. He needed to clear himself, he said. There came no answer, of course. They remained immune to his excuses, immobile to his apologies for being the only human walking. Their cold stares only humiliated Raúl and he left the couple with shame squeezing his thin face.

His shoes echoed loudly in the silence. Before, his steps had covered the ground like the breath of mice, but now their heavy tread made him clutch his small hands together and wince. He gathered his strength to try and convince the angry faces that he was not to blame.

Please, sir," he said to a kindly looking gentleman, "do not think that I have anything to do with this. I swear that I'm ignorant of the cause. I am a humble man, sir. I know nothing of this." The older man stared dispassionately into the distance. "Sir, I beg you." But the man remarked not a bit.

Raúl staggered against a wall and put his hands high over his head. "Oh, God," he said. Raúl's knees buckled and he sank to the ground. He cried, tears falling from his eyes like white beans. It took more than an hour for him to wind his way home from the practice hall. He had paced back and forth with such anxiety that he had passed his violin case several times before finally locating it.

There was no joy in the walk home. He would stop beside a still figure, reach a trembling hand out as if to beg forgiveness, then pull it back to cover his pale face. Dogs and birds remained as they were the instant the world had stopped moving. Dogs fast on the heels of children, a bluejay caught three feet above the pavement. The bird's beak held a small morsel of bread; the bird's body angled away beside an approaching boy wearing tennis shoes and a calculating look.

At his building, Raúl gasped to see Father Domínguez staring sadly into the street. There was interminable longing in those eyes that watched two boys changing a bicycle tire. "Why you?" Raúl asked. He knelt and kissed the Father's cross. "Why did you stop with the others?" He kissed the Father's fingers. "Let me go in your place, Father." Again, no answer came to wrench the confusion from his breast.

Inside the landing, Raúl held the door open to look back. The poor priest's habit, having waved upward in a gust of wind and then having set like meringue, revealed a torn undershirt. Raúl released the door so that it slowly closed on that desolate sight.

He entered and pushed the elevator button, then recoiled in shame. How could he ride the elevator while the world sat still as wood? It was not fair that he should ride when he alone was left to walk. Raúl gripped his collar and turned from the ancient machine. His chin quivered as he stepped up the dust-choked stairs. On the second floor, he heard the metal door of the elevator open and stopped. He shouted with a sudden hope that someone walked in the building, but then remembered the slowness of the elevator. The realization was a renewed pain that became a desperate bird in his chest.

On the sixth floor, Mrs. Delgado leaned against her door. He nearly cried not to hear her jubilant call of "señor Tiny!" Instead, she had an arm raised high, her face partially squinting and the little finger of her raised arm stuck in one ear. Raúl removed his hat and clutched it to his chest. The times of having Mrs. Delgado laugh brightly, look down into his face and give him an encouraging pat on the head were over. "Forgive me," he said, forcing himself toward his door.

Inside, Raúl swore that he would not eat. He stared from the window at the barren street below. No justice in the world would condone his eating. He prayed softly, his forehead pressed against the windowpane. Sunlight came into the room and cast light over the small round table and single chair behind him. Cups and saucers were piled neatly by the sink. A spider hung like a bead over the dishes. On the table, a carefully folded napkin cradled his fork, knife and spoon. Off to one side, a broom so small it seemed more a toy than real was pushed up alongside an equally small mop.

He tried reasoning.

How, indeed, could he be at fault? He knew nothing of what happened. Surely, no one can be blamed for things they know nothing about. But Father Domínguez would not be frozen if things were running as they should. Perhaps this was death. God, in His magnificence, had brought him from the valley and placed him here. Father had never spoken about a heaven like this. Or was it hell? Was he being punished for his weakness? Weren't the weak to inherit the earth? It was all too confusing.

He was alone, that much was certain. Poor Mrs. Delgado. No more music of birds. For some reason, he had been damned. Hell was eternal solitude. But that wasn't so very different from his life before, he thought. No, Raúl knew that whatever fate had befallen him, it was not to eternal shame. He was now free of the suffering for being small, free of the constant ridicule by the giants, the constant reminding through television, magazines and posters that he would never have a lush blonde pining for him because of his size.

Even as the thought came to him, Raúl Sombra began to hum. He stepped away from the window and smiled. Yes, he knew the situation now. He hummed loudly as he opened his violin case.

The bow first urged tentative steps from the strings. Raúl closed his eyes. He pleaded for strength through his chords, became embarrassed by his fears, then walked more boldly out. It was music that ran headlong down the stairs, calling out that he was no different from others. He played to show that he stood eye to eye with them. It was foolish. The excitement ebbed.

Instead, he created small flowers from the strings. He coaxed perfect buds from the violin. They filled the room with a secretive fragrance. But the secretiveness, though perfect in its beauty, isolated him, kept him, as always, unnoticed. "No!" he asserted sharply. He built gardens, then: whole landscapes of trees and bushes, ponds with frogs, women in billowy dresses resting by swings, fountains of violet water, a purple slipper. He stopped. It was a sad fantasy.

The truth is the sadness of the human soul. He played the frailty of human compassion, then. He walked the streets, gazing into windows where people rooted themselves to copy machines and televisors. His playing passed loud women, fat men with sweaty faces, gangs of boys and endless factories. He entered the souls of people with no hope, of people emptied of passion and creaking like barges with the refuse of hopeless concerns. The truth is the sad cry of birds and the patience of insects he played.

Raúl set the violin back in its case and moved to the window again. He pressed his face against the glass and imagined sleeping on the ledge.

Days passed with no change in the world and very little change in Raúl Sombra. He kept his apartment on the sixth floor only to look from the high window. He played at home, now that he was alone. What difference now those scowling faces in the street? One day, he hammered the old paint from the window and opened it. His music floated down into the streets and around the frozen people. He could see the notes encircling now this head, now that child's smiling face. His music entered into the trousers of the city, the pockets of buildings. It filled whole restaurants, entering into the kitchens, the pots, the greased baking pans.

Then he realized he could play as he walked among the statues of ancient giants. He could play as he wanted, without thinking of how this note relied on those traditions, or how his finger at this stop stirred these suggestions. What difference now those scowling faces in the street? Raúl found especially appreciative audiences among the patient citizens of Clowerston. He picked out several of the more compassionate ones and hauled them to the front of his apartment building. There, he arranged them out in the street. Standing beside Father Domínguez, Raúl played for them until late in the evening. Then, with a gracious wave of his hand, he turned and ascended the stairs.

He ate a supper of roast goose late that night, compliments of the local butcher. It was on that first day that he had forgiven himself the oath not to eat. He was not to blame, and God works in mysterious ways. Who was he to question?

Of course, not even Raúl Sombra could remain content indefinitely. There were moments of deep depression. He would refuse to leave his room. He refused to look from the window, and only felt a sickness in his heart like a thick shard. He would refuse to sweep his floor, and took perverse pleasure in allowing dust to settle onto the table, silverware, clothes. The sun spilling into the room gave him no relief. In fact, it only deepened those times of futility.

Hours and even days would pass in this tenor before Raúl would finally gather his wretched bones from the bed and cross to the window. There, he would cry for the immobile world. He would wish to be ridiculed just so others might move about, to hear another voice.

On one such day, he slapped the wall and let the skin of his cheek drag against the window. "Damn it, why?" he cried. His skin squeaked against the glass.

Raúl brought out his violin and played music that made his stomach acidic. He played as if to feel, redoubled, that desolation he felt. He played until he could not stop shaking. And his arms sagged wearily by his sides.

There came a knock at the door. The knock moved slowly into the room.

He stood very still, trying to listen for footsteps or breathing—something that would prove the knock. Another knock came, softer this time.

Raúl placed the violin and bow on his bed. He opened the door to see Mrs. Delgado standing with her arms pressed tightly against her chest, her face streaked with tears. He could say nothing to her.

"I had no idea," she said. "It was beautiful. Beautiful."

"What?"

"Your playing." She cried openly. "You play so beautifully."

Raúl blushed and offered her a handkerchief.

"I'm sorry," she continued. "It's just that I never knew. Oh, Mr. Sombra, it was beautiful. We all think so."

He peered behind her and saw faces looking up from the staircase, staring brightly from doorways. Someone called "Bravo!" and the many faces opened up to carry on the shout.

His ears rang with the sound of applause. He listened intently and heard clapping from each floor of the building. The sounds of cheering filled the room from the window. He moved quickly to look out and saw hundreds of upturned faces calling his name in a deafening roar.

Soon, the revived newspapers proclaimed a new genius. As if from nowhere, they said. One time-honored magazine, with mass-market appeal, had his portrait on the cover and an insightful interview with the legendary Sombra. "The sexiest man in the world," the cover said. Inside, he was quoted as saying, "I practiced every day." The critics gave unreserved praise: The Maestro plays from the most profound depths of human sorrow. Never before has music been played with such passion. And no wonder, they exclaimed with a wink, the diminutive genius could understand the wretched human condition as no other could!

And, as his name swept through the world, so the world swept through Raúl Sombra. He was paid large sums of money to play. Heads of State fought bitterly to have him come and perform in their squares and in their circular rooms. A women's journal of no mean repute named him the eligible bachelor of the year and published articles on how to reject tall men. A renowned architect designed and built a home for Raúl. The mansion held three-hundred rooms, especially equipped for Monsieur Sombra. Large men would sit in fragile chairs and drink tea while waiting for some acknowledgment from the Maestro. Women in expensive dresses brought him gifts and rare cakes, much to the chagrin of their husbands. He knew well enough that it would not last.

Raúl, of course, left the old apartment amid cheers and oaths of love, and never returned, though he did send Mrs. Delgado a Christmas card every year. He had entered a world previously inconceivable to him.

Oh, it was a rare world into which Raúl Sombra had entered. In spite of it, he felt sadness when he recalled the immovable world. He longed, at times—at times not unlike those past depressions—to hear the sound of his own footsteps rising unmolested into the air. He longed for his open window and the mannequins in the streets. He would imagine his passionate and private chords filling boxes tucked away in attics, fluttering like birds in alleys and encircling the pretty ankle of some tranquil woman, the muscled neck of a distraught man.

These times never failed to bring tears to his eyes so that, alone in his mansion, he sometimes wept. And always he carried like a secret pebble lodged in his soul the truth that could never be told. He only hoped that in time it would turn into a pearl. Though that, too, could never be told.

Office Games

Grandmother Xmucane grieved for her two grandsons, even though she was instrumental in their end. It was her failing, as she had said to them, that was the real cause of it. She missed their arts and missed their planting. And she sighed wherever she went, filling up the cracks and the holes in the house with her sighs, packing the ground with the weight of her sighs, the trees bending like old men in from the fields, tumplines full of her sighs.

The twins shouldered their way through them, pressed their way into the house. Xpiacoc visited this mourning to give Grandmother even more to sigh about.

"7 Parrot and his sons have discovered their God within metal," he said. "He calls himself the sun; his wife is the moon."

Blowgunner and Jaguar Sun rose to meet Grandmother's sorrow. "We shall make an end of their boasting," they promised her.

Yet even their victory against Parrot did not make Xmucane's sadness lift. She walked in the fields with her gray head down, her old arms loose or listless. She stood beside the great murals and imagined her missing grandsons carving

and painting, honoring K'ux Kah with artistry. She imagined
a time when such artists could exist freely, a time when there
was a nourisher, a brightener that could subsist in the world
of flesh, without the need of force.

Look, Grandmother," the twins said. "We have planted
corn for you. Don't grieve. We are also your grandchildren.
We can substitute for our older brothers. We've learned a little of their ways, too. Come and look in the fields."

They picked up their axes, their hoes, and each went out
with a blowgun on his shoulder. "At high noon come and give
us our food, Grandmother."

I'll see your work," she answered. Perhaps she was hope-
ful. Perhaps she longed to see just a little of their brothers in
these younger twins.

But in the fields, they just stuck the hoe into the ground
and it worked there by itself. They weren't really ready to be
farmers and fine artists. And their hoe didn't work away by
itself for very long either; there was also an axe. The twins
planted it in the side of a tree and the tree just girdled itself
and felled itself. The axe cut the trees and cleared the brush
from the fields; the hoe set about moving huge amounts of
ground, lifting out innumerable spiny magueys. But that's
not all that the twins did in the field. They also consulted
Dove, there by a big trunk.

"We want you to watch for our grandmother, who is coming to give us food. When she comes along, call out to us so
that we can grab the hoe and axe."

All right," said Dove. "My eyes will be full of wings for
you."

It wasn't farming that Blowgunner and Jaguar Sun were
doing, but making a pretense so that they could hunt birds
with their blowguns in the field and along the river.

When Dove called, they ran quickly. One grabbed the hoe
and one grabbed the axe. They had already wrapped their
heads up and trickily scrubbed soil on their hands. One of
them even dirtied his face as though he were really a farmer;

the other one lifted a wooden post to his head as though he were really a woodcutter. Grandmother stood for a moment overlooking the field and all their imitation work. It was a trick so that Grandmother would come and look and give them their food. So she gave them their food.

Later at home, they arrived complaining: "We're really tired," they said. "This work is hard: making things grow. We never realized."

"No," she said, "you never realized."

They stretched their legs and backs, rubbed their sore feet and callused hands before their grandmother. And the next day they went back to the cornfield. To their surprise, all the trees had risen up again and the bushes, too. The spiny magueys had grown back as they were before their digging.

"Someone is trying to deceive us," they said.

Yet they farmed again the way they had farmed before. They ran along the wooded edge and hunted with their blowguns while the hoe and axe did the tilling and the felling. After their noon meal, they hunted a little more and then took counsel together among the timber and furrows.

"Let's come back and watch over the field in secret," they said. "We'll discover what's happening here at night."

At home, between bites of dinner, between bites of steamed corncakes stuffed with beans and chiles, with the quietness of night rubbing up against the walls, they explained to Xmucane of the reappearance of the land and trees. "Someone must be planning something against us because it was all a great weed patch when we returned. It was a great forest again when we got there. It was as if we had done nothing all day."

"Yes," she said, "it's as if you have done nothing."

"There must be someone doing this."

She ladled the sweet pumpkin sauce. "There must be *something* afoot."

That night, they hid themselves completely in the shadows among the felled trees. As they watched, animals gathered very close to where the twins sat to observe. It wasn't until many of them counseled together that it seemed the animals might act. Finally, in the very heart of the night, they spoke out in sonorous voices, these animals: "Rise, walk, affirm yourself, O tree! Rise, walk, O bush! Overcome!" they said again and again.

Yet it was impossible to see clearly which animals commanded most, which gave the orders, which called up the fallen earth. Then the animals lined up under the trees, under the bushes and appeared suddenly, paired, close to the twins. The first to pass were Panther and Jaguar. The twins reached for them, but failed to grab either one. Next came Deer and Rabbit. The twins lunged after them, too, and managed to pull only a little of their tails. Deer and Rabbit squealed. Their noise frightened the other animals, so that the twins found themselves with no new knowledge, only a little hair in their palms. Finally, a solitary animal came late to the meeting, scurrying down the path to be snared by the twins' anger.

They grabbed Rat and smacked him behind the head. Blowgunner nearly choked the creature, he shook him so hard. Then Jaguar Sun held Rat over a fire to burn every bit of hair from his tail. To this day a rat's eyes and tail are peculiar because of the strangling and the burning that the twins did.

And between gasping for breath, teeth chattering together, Rat said, "Hey, I shouldn't die by you." But these words in the mouth of Rat were like seeds in a calabash because of the way Blowgunner shook him.

"Please," Rat said. "This is not your office, this farming. But you have one! Stop, please."

The twins saw a little humor in the way Rat's small legs whipped back and forth, the way his belly let loose his chattering speech.

"What is our office, then?" Blowgunner said, holding Rat at arm's length: The smell of burned hair was very strong.

Tell us!" Jaguar Sun demanded.

"Let me go so I can talk. I can't speak when you shake me. My word is in my belly, but when you shake me it's as if I'm talking out of three mouths at once."

The sons shook Rat one more time, to impress upon him that they would jumble his bones if he did not speak.

"If you give me a little something to eat," Rat said, "I can dislodge some of these thoughts." He rubbed his stomach.

"Say it now," he was told.

"All right, all right."

The twins released him.

"Your office is the same as your fathers, 1 Blowgunner and 7 Blowgunner. Their gaming things. I know where they are, these rings and the ball. They're laid across the top of the house. All of them: rings, gloves, masks, rubber ball. Your grandmother doesn't show them to you because that was what killed your fathers. She has had enough of sorrow."

How do you know this?" they asked.

"Your fathers went to Xibalbá to play the game, so that is your office, too. Don't you have their names? They played this game with great honor, your fathers. It is your grandmother who has hidden the truth all this time. She asked secrecy from 1 Monkey and 1 Howler."

"Tell us, then."

"I should have something to eat for this telling."

"Tell!"

Rat's ears perked up. "Okay, your fathers dressed like true lords when they played. They wore deer skins and coyote skins on their shoulders, quetzal feathers through their belts. On their arms and legs, they wore leather with jade and turquoise. Their masks sparkled with silver like hoarfrost. And their gloves were embroidered by 1 Monkey and 1 Howler with signs of their greatness. Their playing was a dance to K'ux Kah, my two lords. It was their struggle against Xibalbá."

"And the game?"

"They played with their bodies as if to the rhythms of piping and singing, and moved the ball from one end of the court to the other until it was sent through the rings."

The twins rejoiced greatly when they heard news of the game as Rat told it. They knew instantly that this was something they were born to do. Rat saw the light in their eyes and told them of the ball made of *ulli*, which bounced with nearly as much speed and grace as their fathers when moving in the game.

"Yes," they said, "we've seen this in the paintings and carvings. We've seen our fathers playing skeletons. In our brothers' paintings. We have seen all of this! And heads cut off!"

It's because your fathers died in Xibalbá that 1 Monkey and 1 Howler drew it that way. It is to show the game with the lords of Hell, and how your fathers were defeated. They lacked trickery and cruelty. But listen, it is also to show how you must play against these lords. The game is Great Honor. The game against those others is not over yet."

"You have spoken well, Rat. The nourishment in your belly is good."

So they gave Rat his food, and this is what his office became: corn, squash seeds, chile, beans, cacao and chocolate. All this rats eat.

"We have seen this game," the two sons said as Rat ate. "We are the substitutes for our fathers, aren't we? We are ballplayers and the sons of ballplayers, Blowgunners and the sons of Blowgunners."

Then they spoke again to Rat. "So this is what is yours: If anything is hidden away in the garbage and you ferret it out, it is yours. You may eat it. You have done us well."

"Is there anything else I may say, my lords?"

"Yes. You will help us get the things from the rooftop. You will help us deceive our grandmother."

"But what should I say if your grandmother sees me?"

"Don't lose heart, we'll be there. We'll know what is to be told to our grandmother. We'll put you up in the eaves of the house and when it is clear, go at once to where the gaming things are. We'll see you signaling us in the house lashings, only it will be in our stew that we will watch for you."

The next day, the sons worked again, but this time they told Grandmother not to bring food to them. Instead, Blowgunner and Jaguar Sun came home for their meal. Rat was held close and hidden as they brought him to the house. It was so Grandmother would have no idea of their deception. Jaguar Sun went right into the house while Blowgunner went to the roof. Quickly, he put Rat up above.

"Just fix our dinners," Jaguar Sun said. "We want chile sauce, Grandmother. With lots of soup. We're very hungry."

She fixed them their dinner as they sat and waited. And when finally she placed a bowl before each of them, they knew they had placed their trick well. They ate the hot stew slowly and finished off their water jug.

"Grandmother," they said, holding out the jug, "this is the best stew yet. It's made us thirsty. Please bring us something to drink."

"All right," she said, and filled their jug from a large urn in the house.

They went on eating, but it wasn't really that they were hungry or thirsty. They looked on the surface of the chile stew and saw Rat curled around the ball, waiting. They wanted Grandmother to have her back toward them as they looked into the stew mirrors before them. And when they found Rat, they released Mosquito to wing his way into the house and prick a hole through the front of the urn. The water streamed out onto Grandmother's foot.

Look at this!" she said, showing them the leak.

"What is it?" they asked.

She tried to seal up the hole.

"We're burning up with thirst. Your stew is too good."

"The urn is leaking."

"Then go to the river. We can't eat this dinner without water. Go to the river if you have to."

They sent her away just as Rat scratched free the ball, so that it fell from the lashings together with the rings, gloves and apron. Quickly, they took them outside and ran down the road to the ball court and hid them. They quickly returned to their meal and waited for Grandmother, but she took so long that they went to the river to see what might have happened. Both their mother and grandmother were busy trying to mend the front of the jug. Each of the twins had his blowgun when they got to the river.

"Won't you wait?" asked Grandmother.

"We got tired of waiting," they said.

Blood Woman shook her head. "It won't be sealed up."

So the twins sealed it with bird's wax. "It's just our magic," they said, beaming with cleverness.

Grandmother clasped her hands together. "Oh, yes," she said, "it is just your magic."

The sons jostled each other. They laughed, then went off in front of their grandmother and mother.

Xmucane stood back and watched them, her hands now to her mouth, her eyes darkening slowly as the boys walked further away in the direction of the valleys, the lowlands. She watched them quietly, no muscle quivering, even as the twins gave a final wave. She stood even longer listening to the sons' laughter rising out from the woods, Blood Woman swishing the jug through the river, the water slapping the sides of the jug as it was lifted to the bank. The cry of a hawk spiraled high above.

"Aren't you coming?" Blood Woman asked.

But Xmucane stood alone, watching the descent of her grandsons, her progeny. She stood watching and thinking. Because this was the disposition of the ball. And of the game.

Mything Linda in the High Window

Finally, after finding a table in the Hyacinthium of the Morrison Hotel, after ordering from the awkward young waiter who just could not get even a simple "mai-tai" and "orgasm" right—who nearly cracked the bowl of mixed nuts in his enthusiasm—and after the first sip and glance around the room, Lori's mother unpinned her chartreuse hat and placed it in the chair beside her and resumed.

"The sky floated above the hills then." Her fingernails clicked against her glass. "The moon ballooned up at night and slipped from ledge to ledge of wispy cloud. I remember the night most of all, there at Los Zorros. The night and Linda Waincox, that is." She flicked her wrist affectedly.

Lori swirled her mai-tai.

"Ours was a town of some forty ranching families, settlers along the once famous creek bed of Bienarto Run. Much smaller than Clowerston. Every season, herds passed by Los Zorros as they had for nearly a hundred years, except that even then many drives had disappeared because of trucking and land sales. The creek running north of town once had the reputation for being the most dangerous stop of any drive in Texas. Ragged trailmen would throw themselves into the creek with all their clothes on. Campfires burned ten feet into the air, and whiskey and cards came out with the usual male loudness. Tale upon tale decorates Zorro Creek." She glanced around for the pert young waiter, but quickly forgot him. "Legend has it that Wyatt Earp, passing through that part of Texas, cleaned it up and turned it into a town where a new breed of rancher lived. The whorehouse and still were torn down, houses went up and men settled with women where before no respectable woman would dare show her face.

"The first house built was a huge white mansion owned by a Colonel Sherman—no relation to *the* Sherman. The house still rose proudly up when I lived there, although the Sherman family rarely occupied it. The large white pillars seemed never to need painting, and the double wood door stood deadly serious for many years. For two of those years the house lay completely empty. Then, in the mild summer of my eleventh year, the Waincoxes moved in."

She leaned forward for effect. "Realize that Los Zorros might have seemed a strange and mysterious place back then. With men and older boys gone for most of the year—in spurts of up to five weeks—and the younger boys lying low in the plain or deep in the creek, the town remained a woman's town. Any stranger there would feel an odd unsettling with the gradual discovery of no males."

Lori raised her glass to click it against her mother's.

"One can never know the truth in a mother's story," she said with a wink, "but my mother once told me about a time— very early in the town's history—when four men happened upon Los Zorros. Dusty men. Spurs and such. Manly men, no doubt, with names like Tom Harold or Bill James. You know two first male names. When these fellows discovered that there weren't any adult males in the town, they decided to be uncivil. Mother used to describe their terrible grins better than I can—'like black caterpillars skulking over bone,' she'd say.

"Well, the younger women were the first to be harassed, of course. The older women approached the brutes and told them that menfolk stayed around only long enough to procreate. Then they were killed and eaten. The men didn't believe a word, naturally—they never do. But, in the middle of the night, as if driven by some silent tradition, the women banded together with broomsticks and mop handles, and crept up the mud-streaked stairs to the room. I always imagine the quietness and the shadows accentuating their broad faces. The women smashed open the door, screaming at the top of their lungs.

"The look on the men's faces as they rode from town gave them something to discuss for years to come. Rather than worry their husbands, though, the women agreed never to tell of the strangers. Only the women would know of this secret well of strength. They made a pact, as they burned the men's belongings in the street. The sound of hoofbeats could be heard over the plain until late in the night. Some said the hoofbeats and mad whipping of horses could be heard on certain nights for years later, but only by women, and once a month. Who's to know?

"Anyway, Lori, the town spread out in the shape of a guitar from the creek. Several homes circled the rough square, more homes faced each other like a neck from the creek, and finally the larger houses poked into the range with their long porches and majestic fronts like tuning pegs of a guitar. The Sherman mansion was at the very head of the town, but instead of facing inward, the white front commanded an impressive view of the open range.

"Herds were driven northward the length of town, first passing the Sherman place and, lastly, through Zorro Creek. The wives set out tables with lemonade for their boys and beer for their men. As each man passed, he would ride up, hug his family and drink. The creek was no longer the night stop of tradition, so the males drank and rode on, many not even getting down from their horses. But the occasion was a grand one. The women paid homage to men and the hard work they did."

"Yeah," Lori said.

"Thirteen-year-old boys, out for the first time, were given special attention and treated to their first beer as if they had gone out and come back full-grown men. Sister Loyola always stood on a rock and gave the Lord's blessing to the drive, and to our men.

"Penny, Rose and I enjoyed the drives even more than our games by the white mansion. For three years we had been gathering by the Sherman home to watch the boys ride in. We would choose the boy of our dreams and pretend we waited for husbands. We watched our mothers bustling around, their bosoms rising and falling in mysterious excitement. One time, Penny wore a tee-shirt beneath her dress so that her chest would seem bigger. Her mother noticed it before the boys arrived and made her take it off. She told her it was too hot. We were ten, then. Your daughter's age. Thank God you divorced that first lunatic! Oscar, wasn't it?"

"You know better."

Lori's mother glanced at the awkward waiter as he brought cocktails to a table of women beside them.

"Shall I run a tab?" he asked them.

The woman in a gray suit answered firmly. "No. Bring me the bill."

The nervous young man left quickly.

"Well," Lori's mother continued, "earlier that particularly mild summer, after Rose turned eleven, our mothers had decided to get us together." She savored her drink slowly before changing her voice to fit the characters.

"'There comes a time,' Penny's mother proclaimed, 'when your body will change, girls.' She was the spokesman for our mothers. 'It's difficult to explain, and often girls your age hear things from other girls and misunderstand what will happen. That's why we've decided to tell the three of you at the same time.' She smoothed down her awful green dress. And then she added, 'I'm telling you the way my mother told me.'

"We knew exactly what she was talking about. We had heard older girls speak elusively of their 'visitor.' The mixture of fantastic rumors and half-truths frightened and embarrassed us.

"'Your body is a temple,' she said."

"No!" Lori said.

"God's truth. 'A temple which must be taken care of properly. Soon, you will all become young women and with that, you'll have very special feelings inside you, but you'll still be too young to understand them.' She sat in a plump blue chair, her hands folded together. 'God created woman to accompany man, taking from Adam a rib and, in His majesty, created both a companion and a wife for him. As wife, Eve had certain obligations toward Adam. Among them was the pleasure of giving children.'"

"God help us!" Lori blurted out.

But her mother continued without laughter. "I looked at my mother in her tan blouse. She smiled, her head tilting to one side. I dared not look at Penny or Rose, but turned back to Mrs. Cummings.

"'At that time, people married much earlier than we do now,' she explained. 'Still, a girl's body reaches womanhood about the same time as Eve reached it. Those special feelings you'll have are special because they teach you the patience to serve your husband in a Godly way. But once you become a young woman in body, you will go through periods of uncleanliness. During those times, and they happen once a month, girls, you will flush out all the poisons in your body so that you'll remain pure and decent the rest of the time.'

"I twisted in my seat, but felt my mother's eyes warning me not to get impatient. Yes, Mrs. Cummings could go on and on.

"'Don't be afraid when it happens,' she said, 'but leave from wherever you are and come to one of us or any of the

women, and we'll talk again and show you what to do.' She
stopped and looked over her knuckles at us. I wanted to say
'yes,' but wasn't sure if she had finished or not. 'Do you understand?' she suddenly asked. I nodded. 'Okay, that's all, children.'

"I remember hearing Rose's mother say, 'Well done,
Mary,' as we walked out of the room."

Lori smiled briefly under her mother's straight-faced
account.

"Of course, our mothers only succeeded in creating a
worse fear than we already had. The poisons took on inordi-
nate proportions. We wanted to know where and how these
poisons would be flushed out. We wanted to know if we could
remain as girls. Could womanhood, somehow, be prevented?
We were altogether too embarrassed and confused to ask the
older girls what this thing was. I remembered back then that
Sandy and Christina stayed at home at times even when there
were dances or picnics. I remembered the look, the bowed
head, the one eyebrow raised between mothers. I remembered
that boys and fathers never spoke about any of this.

"So, all this came together the summer of our eleventh
year. The floating sky seemed nailed to the hills the night
Linda moved in, as if her arrival linked itself with that town,
that configuration of hills, the endless plain and those manly
drives in some portentous way—I'm quite serious, Lori. I
remember that Penny looked at me and said, 'She could have
been our age!' It felt like a lost opportunity when we learned
she had recently turned thirteen. We wanted another girl-
friend. Safety in numbers, or something. Her age, though,
seemed less an obstacle than the fact that for three weeks she
never came outside.

"We still played by the side of the mansion, looking out
over the range while pretending we were pioneer women, but
then half our interest in playing came from a curiosity about
this new girl. Linda's room looked out both the front and east
sides of the house. During the day, we could see light from the

range-side filtering through both curtains to spill lightly down the town-side of that white-washed house. From the ground, looking up to the second story, we saw her lacey white curtains and beige ceiling. Strange azaleas grew from the window box on the east side. The pink flowers reached up past the sill."

"Pink azaleas in window boxes!?"

Lori's mother waved off her disbelief.

"Occasionally, we glimpsed Linda standing by the glass with her hand peeling back the curtain. She looked lonely with her piercing gaze and long blonde hair hanging straight down her back. Sometimes she leaned out, glass pitcher in hand, to water the flowers. Her skin, white like undyed linen, blended perfectly with the wall. Her lips were as naturally red as cochineal.

"Three weeks after she moved in, Linda stepped from her house. We swung on Mrs. Wilson's porch swing and watched her walk by. She walked with her mother, both of them dressed in long summer dresses with cream-colored bows in their hair. Linda wore patent leather shoes that didn't creak.

"'She looks pretty,' Rose said.

"'She looks like a snob,' Penny answered.

"Rose smiled uncomfortably, so I said, 'Let's ask her to play.'

"'She's too good to play with us. Why should she stay inside for so long?'

"Penny's question made me think of the mysterious 'visitor,' but I didn't say anything because Penny suddenly jumped from the swing with excitement.

"'Let's follow them,' she said.

"We waited until they had gone several houses down, then we ran along the boardwalk and between the houses to spy. Mrs. Waincox steered Linda toward the Thomas home. 'She's going to meet Sandy,' Rose said. We waited across the street by a garden fence."

Lori's mother suddenly twisted in her seat. "Waiter!" She motioned for him to bring a menu: She mimed opening a large menu and reading the selection and choosing something with her finger springing straight up. The waiter finally understood. "He's a slow one, isn't he?

"Anyway, evidently, Linda was receiving the grand tour of the town because she no more than met Sandy when they left to call at another house. We followed with more enthusiasm. At the end of the long trip, around the instrument of town, Linda's mother stopped at Mrs. Adamson's grocery. The three of us had been following on the boards when we saw them stop. Penny motioned for us to come around the neighboring house. We ran around and, thinking they would be inside, burst from the corner and right beside them.

"Mrs. Waincox laughed. 'So, here're the three Bremens,' she said. 'We thought you had given up.' She beamed down and asked our names. Penny introduced us. 'That's nice,' she said. 'This is Linda, and I'm Mrs. Waincox.' Linda smiled. 'Talk to the girls while I go inside.' Linda's mother patted my head as she moved into the store.

"'Hi,' Penny said.

"Linda smiled again, her green eyes moist.

"A slight breeze swirled around us. It lifted the ruffles of our dresses. It grazed our foreheads and pushed hair behind our shoulders like a friend's finger as she whispers a secret."

"Mother!" Lori said in surprise, "you're such a good story-teller!"

"Hush, now. 'Why didn't you come out at first?' Penny asked abruptly.

"'What do you mean?' Linda asked.

"'You never came out until now.'

"'Oh,' she said, 'I was sick from the trip. Momma didn't want me to go out and give it to anyone else.'

"I wondered if the change could be communicable?"

Lori chuckled.

"'Are you really thirteen?' asked Rose.

"Linda looked us over carefully. 'Yes. How old are you?'

"'We're all eleven,' Penny said.

"'That's nice.'

"We stared at each other and then pretended that we weren't staring at each other. Rose leaned her head against Penny's shoulder. Mrs. Waincox came out with a small brown bag and took Linda away. Before they left, she gave each of us a mint drop.

"As soon as they were out of earshot, Penny lifted her shoulder to her chin and said, 'That's nice.' We laughed at her imitation of Linda. Even her mother said it. Penny posed again. 'That's nice,' she said." Lori's mother affected both of the voices with her fingers scribbling the air.

"We played very little with Linda, probably as much because she didn't want to play with girls two years younger than her as we had, by Penny's teasing, named Linda an outsider."

The waiter stepped alongside the table. "There you are, ma'am." He leaned beside Lori and smiled as he placed menus in front of them. "Shall I bring another drink?"

"Later." Lori's mother ordered him off with a wave.

"Late summer—the mild summer—came and the drive brought our men back. A few days before, we overheard from some older girls that Linda had started her womanhood and would not be joining the celebration. It would have been her first. We were shocked. Penny asked Christina what it was like. Penny, being the oldest, was quickly losing her inhibitions and questioned openly. Christina made a face and said, 'It hurts and you bleed all over everything.' Penny looked like she had a dentist appointment as Christina left. Slowly, fearfully, Penny turned to us. 'Poor Linda,' she said.

"I helped my mother arrange a table with beer and beef jerky. Penny and Rose came later, with their mothers and younger brothers. Sister Loyola walked solemnly to her rock and stood with her gaze steadied out over the plain. Her hat folded down against one ear in the wind. Her cross swung against her chest, then caught beneath her arm. Penny, Rose and I moved over in front of the Sherman mansion to wait. Above us, Linda's window opened. She stood close to the curtain, her delicate hand holding the soft material. She never looked down, but instead stared out like a figure on the prow of a ship.

"Then, with a shrill cry, Sister Loyola signaled the approaching men. The air sprang to life with excitement, like a sudden rain of cicadas. Wives hurried to make sure tables were set just right. They smoothed their hair and patted their faces, then turned southward. A dust cloud rolled forward over the range. Gradually, the whoops and hollers of men keeping order among the animals reached our ears. I suspect we all breathed hard then, waiting to see the brave men ride in with dust flying from their jeans, hats waving wildly, manly hoots and cheers rising above them.

"Penny reached for us in her excitement, and grabbed our arms. 'Ooh,' she said, 'I would do anything for a kiss from Richard Edgar.' Rose and I could only giggle with embarrassment.

"As we squirmed, the first armadillos padded by. Dust from their legs swirled shallowly around their faces. Their shells bumped and clicked like walnuts. Rose squealed as a great cheer burst from the waiting women. The experienced boys led the drive, followed by the first-timers—Richard among them—and the men last. One little dogey bolted from the herd and ran toward us. Before we could react, we heard a loud 'he-ya!' and saw Richard Edgar spur his mount after the stray. He slapped his hat against his thigh, sending dust in a spray around him, and drove the balled-up armadillo back to the herd with a manly punt of his foot.

"Armadillos?" Lori asked.

"We hurrahed and clapped for him. When Richard dismounted, he bowed, his face red with a shy pride, but instead of looking at us, he lifted his handsome face to smile up at the window over our heads. We looked at Linda in the high window, dressed in pink, one hand holding the white curtain aside, her blonde hair partially pinned so her long curls cascaded down her shoulder. We saw the whiteness of her smile, the delicateness of her skin, and knew that she was a woman now, a real woman. In her radiant smile, we saw our futures, too: the wonderful change coming for each of us. A change that could make a Richard Edgar turn red and show off. A change that would make a girl suddenly frail and beautiful in a high window, like a picture in a strange frame of some fairy tale!"

Lori's mother finished off her drink and swirled the glass in her fingers. "A change," she gave as denouement, "that could be to a young heart like a mother's emotional kiss in the death of night when the sound of prowling men comes boisterously up from the street."

"Is that true?" Lori asked. She poked her mai-tai with the umbrella.

Lori's mother nodded gravely. "Oh, yes," she said. "Oh, yes, indeed." She opened the menu. Her eyes ducked behind the large and leathery menu, then suddenly sparkled over the top edge. "Shall we have the Key-lime pie? Another drink? Steak?"

Lori laughed. "Armadillo steaks?"

Cassandra's eyes twinkled. "Let's ask the waiter."

Lori smiled and shook her head. "No, Mother, he'll get in trouble. The poor boy."

"Do you think he'll ask the chef?"

They looked over at the young man, standing awkwardly by the wall, a white napkin in his hands, the faintest moustache coloring his face. He would be quite a handsome man if he kept a certain frailty. And if his complexion cleared up.

Lori signaled for him.

"That's the spirit," her mother said. "Never give them a break."

The News of The Author

"The news of the building of the wall
now penetrated into this world,"
— Franz Kafka.

Finally, the news reached us about The Murder. The dark glove of its fame spread across the country, covering the landscapes between empires with its coarse weave. Of course, there was no other like it. Like so many other stories of hands or reach, or extensions beyond any grasp of reason, this, too, arrived late to our village. Not so late that we had already poured out our Pho and stock pots, but we had been eating molded bread for as long as my son had been alive. Yet, in this, we were hardly different from hundreds of other villages scattered along the waterways, the roads. We lived far from the Imperial throne.

I remember the boatman, dark-draped, black-hatted, poling along the softer currents in the very center of the river. He waved and called excitedly. All of us ran to the bank to receive him. The officials from my union stood back. It was a premonition, I suppose, thick as fog in our heads. Our leader, the distinguished assassin of several difficult marks, stood with his hands clasped behind his back. His long, bound hair seemed a sable muffler draped over his shoulder. The blood-red ribbon at the end stood boldly out against his black pajamas. I held my son's hand. He had already killed, much to my delight. He was to be initiated into the union in the coming month. Already he had our desperate look, our hunger for recognition, our talk of higher visions, our ravenous grip.

Our mayor went down the slippery bank to receive the boatman. The mud and slickered vines made it difficult for both men. They had to embrace to keep from falling. Yet the man would only give the news to the president of our union. Our leader nodded. He wrapped his braid several times around his neck like a necklace and made his cautious way down. By this time the boatman had returned to the safety of his launch. Our leader met him on board. The waves rocked it gently, so they spoke quickly but comfortably. The men shook hands, embraced and then the boatman left to carry the news farther on. Our leader stood facing away from us. Was he hiding his reddened eyes? He did not wave, but watched contemplatively the river swells, the current swirls, and the long poling barge disappearing toward the next village.

He would not share with the others the intimate words of the messenger until he had addressed the union first. There was no amount of coaxing to wheedle it from him. He was resolute.

Our lodge is the best along this stretch of the river. We have electricity and typewriters. The walls and aisles have towering bookshelves. These, of course, are overcrowded with mysteries, with who-dunits. They are impossibly crammed vertically and horizontally so that it can be most difficult to locate a particular volume. It is a library we are very proud of and, indeed, it must be acknowledged that we take turns dusting this interminable labyrinth of shelves. Not one of us would dare complain about our duties—what is there to complain about? Our lives are good. Furthermore, each of us has worked late through the night on some plot or another—

culling the references—and each of us knows the cycle of the
evening. The lamps and soft electric lights call forth the
moths. The dying ones bring the toads. With their quick
tongues, they devour only those flapping over the earthen
floor. Early morning, half an hour before daybreak, the chickens enter and finish the dead moths. By six in the morning
the long night of hunger and duty, with its litter of corpses, is
nowhere to be seen. It is as if there had been no struggle at all
during the wee hours, the blind hours.

"This is what the boatman said to me," our leader began.
He stood at the podium, his arms outstretched, his hair loose
and flowing to below his waist. He held his arms out and
there were none of his traditional ribbons, ties, broaches or
jewelry. He wore a white tunic and left his hair unbound. He
had kept himself as unadorned as the most devout acetic for
the news.

"'Finally,'" our leader continued, "'we can rest.' This is
what the boatman said to me. 'Finally, The Murder has been
committed. Little is known of The Author except that The
Murder was done in our empire's capital—as it should be—
protected by the barbarian wall, and there he has accom-
plished what we have all longed for. But there is no
knowledge of whether The Author is one of us or someone
brought from outside the wall. We do not even know if it is a
man or a woman. If there are children for this genius. Finally,
all we know is that The Murder has occurred.'" And then he
bowed deeply before us, religiously; his great cascade of hair
fell like a black cowl about his shoulders and face.

He then thrust up and—wild! horse mane!—swept his
long tresses back in an arc over his head. We were beyond
gasping.

We understood this and still understand it, even though
we are so far from the center of the empire that we have yet
to receive details of The Murder. But the news was for us,
after all, this: The Author's final coming. After all, there were
many in the village who hardly bothered with the deaths we

orchestrated. Others complained that we still had not quite got it right, that there was more that needed to be done, that we got near but not quite home to the authentic. Some openly disdained our butcherings as banal, unimaginative. And there were those who berated us for our apparent self-indulgent life. What did we give to our village? We killed our fellow villagers, imperfectly; we maimed and tortured to fulfill abstruse notions that only we subscribed to. We lived our lives simultaneously crying about the present and looking to some distant time beyond our meager lives when posterity would recognize our talents, our teeth. For generations beyond recollection, we, in our union, suffered attacks of apathy. And now, finally, The Author made all our travails bearable. The Murder had come to exonerate us, but not only us—everyone who lived! The Author was the arrow leading us into light.

Who knows? Perhaps The Murder, once it is finely explicated—did I say that the details haven't yet reached our village?—will bring a new purpose for our carnage. Perhaps we will be able to imitate this oeuvre nonpareil with innumerable permutations. Perhaps our small homicides will be analyzed as precursors, as earlier forms of the great evolutionary state of The Murder. Perhaps we will be asked to formulate opinions, to help decipher the less obvious conceits of the work. Perhaps a new age of cultural critique will begin, where practitioners—instead of non-practitioners—will be seen as the experts.

Wild! Horse mane! Arc of the tresses—black optimism and freedom!

We all wear white tunics now. We all do: Hierophants of steel. Some, in our union, have perfected a knowing smile that lingers across our lips like the faint grins on maple leaves.

The English Professor

Thursdays are a kind of game for us. We sit at Gwynne's to drink beer because it is the only place—after our careful and particular combing of Clowerston — with just the right environment. We feel free enough to speak of intellectual matters and, yet, the place has a decent coterie of street people. Albert Heinz is the living Gwynne's to me. I never really stop to ask myself why it is I've befriended him except to note that we both have an urge to range our conversations from a sincere investigation into aspects of human behavior to an appreciation of the assets of several young women. He has read a great deal for a businessman. Besides, I like the way he sucks his beer bottle to produce a popping sound at the end of his drink. I have never been able to do it in all the years we've known each other.

We had been drinking and eating pretzels for some time already. We talked about our wives, the children, and God knows what else when, with both of us slightly drunk, we began reminiscing about our undergraduate days at Indiana University. It started like all nostalgic conversations: slowly at first, with laughter as common bonds were recalled; then we moved on to more private and poignant memories. I don't know why I wanted to tell him about Professor Halstead. It had been a long time since I'd thought of him. I admired him. No, it was stronger than that. I loved the man. There. Said and done.

Albert ordered another round for us.

"Remember Professor Halstead?" I asked. It was rhetorical as we both knew that he had no connection with the English Department. Al had slipped away into the business school his freshman year.

"No."

"He taught English literature. Probably the best teacher in the department. I don't know if he did anything that was important in the field, but everyone loved his classes."

"Uh-huh," he said. He would be patient for a bit.

"He made his points very clear, encouraged discussion, and made us all enthusiastic—you know, thinking about things we had never thought about before: life, the heart, etc. But I never heard about his being a great or even good scholar."

He sucked his beer.

"I've never run across an article by him."

"Strange," he said, lobbing me a pitch for the sake of moving the story forward.

"Not really. There're so many of us, and so many journals, that it's impossible to keep up. Anyway, I can remember the whole class watching him as if he were a guru. Everything he said filled us with a wonder for literature, and for the creative minds of writers. If I hadn't declared my major when I first had him, I would have with that class."

"He played his role well."

"Yes: Al, the cynic. But you're right, he did. It was beautiful. When I started teaching, I wanted to be just like him. I wanted to do what he did to students. You know?"

Al fidgeted with his coaster.

"He was good-looking, too. Always wore a sport coat and tie; spoke in a kind of Oxford professor's voice. He had an informality, though."

Al looked at me with one eyebrow raised.

"That's a game, too, I know, but one listened to him out of a fascination with his appearance, his personality and, of course, the ideas he offered to us." I sipped my beer. "A good-looking man. Wore his hair just slightly long. Combed roughly, and carelessly."

"I didn't know you noticed those things," he said, sneering behind his beer. "Or is it that all English professors are really frustrated writers?"

"Have your fun, have your fun. You had your turn, so now it's mine."

"Okay." He lit a cigarette and blew a smoke ring with careful deliberation. "But no boring crap."

"He had very dark hair and dark, dark eyes. Eyes that were black through and through. And I don't just mean the pupils, but everything. His eyes were white, of course, but with deep, black pits."

"Weak description, Naranjo."

"Go to hell. His eyes ..."

"Yes, his eyes."

"His eyes were black. But in the dead center of those black wells ..."

"There shone the glimmer of an intellectual force quite unique and mysterious!" Al saluted the air with his bottle.

"There were two spots of burgundy red. Like a cat, almost. Not yellow, or white, but red light." I waited for the image to sink into his hard head.

"All the time, Naranjo?" He hummed a piece of the *The Twilight Zone* song. "Surely not. It was the light, right?"

"With just a touch of silver in his hair."

He pushed back in his seat. "All right, so you're going to make stuff up as you go along."

"Truth," I said.

"Right."

"When he explicated a story or novel, we gave him absolute attention. No, he drew it out of us. Against our wills. He made us see just how ingeniously written each piece was. We read Conrad, Dostoevsky ..."

"Christ, I don't know anything about them."

"But his favorite authors were Kafka, Poe and Borges. He liked those authors because they tackled a similar—and singular—effect through different means. Each of them seemed to create, for lack of a better word, a Zen koan state through his writing. They weren't concerned with a variety of effects or a sine wave of responses from the reader—like the novelists we, ah, like novelists—but they were concerned with a suspension of reason and emotion at an instance when both reason and emotion reached the same heightened level, yet both proved deficient in grasping the world."

Al stared coldly at me. "If you give me a lecture, I'll spray beer on you."

"Sorry. No, I won't. The thing is that he spun intricate and convincing theories about each author. We came from his classes speechless and filled with new insights into literature and the nature of human creativity."

"Please," he said, rolling his eyes.

"All right." I took a drink. "There was this girl."

"Finally! A plot!"

"She always sat next to me. We talked." I caught Al's look. "Just talked." He shrugged. "It happened that we did get to know each other later, but that's irrelevant."

"Uh-huh."

"It turned out that we had different ideas about what was going on in class."

"That's par for the course."

"Let me tell the story, okay?"

"Go ahead." He took a gulp, and popped his bottle. "But I won't believe anything you say."

"Cassandra and I always sat next to each other in class. It was 'Literary Interpretation.' We were both English majors, so the course was required. The first day, though, we knew that this would be different. Most required courses are bad, right? We talked about that: how being forced into something makes us rebel, etc. It developed our, well, our acquaintanceship. Something about sitting together, thighs lightly touching.... Whew! I must be getting drunk. I'm talking about things that don't matter. Is the effect lost on you?"

"Nice try, Naranjo."

"Ah, well. Anyway, the first couple of weeks, we were floored by this guy. Everything he did amazed us. People who missed classes in other courses never missed his. He had a strange way of walking back and forth at the front of the room, gesturing and pausing dramatically. Sometimes, I would get entranced by his actions and drift away from what he was actually saying, but it never lasted long because what he related was interesting. He unraveled the intricate lies of this author or that passage, pointed out the unreliable narrators, and revealed the hidden worlds. By the third week, he had us completely trained. When he entered the room, everyone stopped talking. His usual trick was to enter amid the reverence, put his papers down on the podium and look up at us. He smiled and then said something trivial, which instantly made us all realize our tense state. There would be a ripple of laughter, and then a comfortable attendance to his words. Each day he said something different, I think. Maybe he had us so well-trained that he actually said the same things, but we loved him so much that it sounded different. Who knows? The effect was the same. It doesn't matter, then." I raised my glass. "Cheers."

"Cheers."

"Being the studious fellow that I am, I read ahead of the assignments. There was the desire to read ahead, too, just to be in his good graces—even though he could have no idea that I was doing it. You know what I mean?"

"Yes."

"It was an urge to please him, as if he could read our minds. I suppose I felt that he *could* read my mind. He read the works with such insight and subtlety that it seemed perfectly natural to assume that he understood each of us simply by bringing to bear that piercing gaze of his. His eyes fell upon each of us in the class—there must have been nearly a hundred students—like a gentle benediction. At least once in every class, he looked directly into the eyes of each and every student. After class, I could hear the girls fairly swoon over him. And, of course, it would have been impossible for me to speak with him after the hour. At the bell, the girls would scurry down the steps and chirp for his attention. During those times—and I always stayed after class to watch this phenomenon—he would smile with the kindness of a saint and direct his complete attention on the individual. It was during one of those scenes that I first wished to be like him. It started as hatred for the students who swarmed down and adored him so openly. I resented them for being so childish, so disrespectful. He had better things to do. Then I realized that it was sheer jealousy that stirred in me. I hated the other students because they had the courage and honesty to go down those steps and huddle around him in awe. Yes, I felt awed by him. And, consequently, too inferior to ever speak with him. I found myself staying later and later to watch him deal with that pilgrimage. I wanted to be like him. The way his patience endured, the way his eyes never tired, or stopped gently touching each waifish soul before him."

"It brings tears to my eyes," Al said.

I chuckled. "And it gets worse."

"Oh, God." He searched the darkness for the waitress, and summoned her to the table. "Want another beer?"

"Sure."

The waitress raised two fingers close to her face. Al nodded.

I drank the little bit from my glass, then poured the remaining drops in the bottle.

"Cassandra and I talked about him the first few times we got together after class. It came as no great surprise, actually. The curious thing came when she talked about him with her eyes wandering to the top of her head. She spoke in that dreamy state about his body."

"Of course."

"The way she spoke, you could see that she fantasized about him. Her elbows would get closer to her sides, her head would tilt just so, as if he were running a soft finger along the line of her chin. If I hadn't thought so much of Halstead, I would have been jealous. As it was, I understood. But when she said her favorite problem in class was losing her train of thought to wallow in his salubriously green eyes, I was stunned. 'Green eyes?' I asked her. 'They're so strong and vigorous,' she said. 'Vigorous!' 'Salubrious!'—those were her words!"

"A-ha!" Al said. "Red eyes, indeed!" He raised his finger in mock detection.

"I let it go the first time because she was so obviously in love with him. The imagination of an eighteen-year-old girl must be allowed free rein."

"Cheers, to that!"

"But, I guess, the thing about green eyes bothered me more than I thought. I started paying very close attention to what he looked like and how he acted. I was still amazed by his lectures and by the way he answered questions, but for a time I paid most attention to his behavior. To accentuate moments when he was deep in thought, he would carefully place the tip of his index finger against his nostrils. He had a definite pattern in his walking, too. The first couple of questions thrown out to the class inevitably came from the right side of the room. He would slide over to the left side by the time the second answer came. There, he would pause with his index finger and thumb of his left hand up to his mouth before continuing with his comments. Several minutes later, he would raise another question. This time, he would smile broadly and clasp his hands behind his back, rising slightly on his toes. I became so good at predicting his behavior that I could almost tell what the questions would be. Of course, his questions were always better and more astute than any I could ever come up with.

"I was particularly deep in concentration over his actions, and paying little attention to what he was saying, when Cassandra nudged me. I looked up and noticed that she had painted her face differently. She could look very good when she wanted to. So, she bent her face close to mine and smiled with one mischievous eye still on Halstead. 'I'm going down after class to speak with him,' she said. I simply nodded, but she continued. 'I'd like to run my fingers through that gorgeous blond hair.' Her eyes never left the man. I looked at her as if she were teasing me, and she smiled. I laughed quietly. 'Let's get together after class, okay?'" She agreed, but warned me that it could be some time. We were to meet in the school commons. Foolish as it was, I assumed that Cassandra was color-blind."

Al laughed loudly. "Black to blond! That's blind, all right!"

"I was young."

"And not too bright."

"And not too bright." I popped a piece of pretzel into my mouth. "I waited, as usual, to watch the downsweep of girls to the front of the room. Cassandra was one of those women that can look so nice walking away. Well, when we finally got together, all she talked about was Halstead. The funny thing is that I went along so easily. I even caught myself imitating his manner once in a while. Cassandra would speak and I would wait with my hand against my mouth in exactly the same way he did. She laughed and pointed it out to me. She said it was adorable. I actually liked what she said."

"That's perverse."

"Well, wait. I really wanted to be like him. Whenever I saw him in the hallways, I would follow him a short way to see how he walked, talked, and everything. Don't laugh, but around mid-term, I went out and bought a sport coat."

"I don't know if I can take much of this."

"No tie, though. That was too much even for me, I guess. Like I said, Cassandra and I did get to know each other, if you know what I mean. Not all the time, but fairly often. I can remember one day—we had been together several times already—when we were lying side by side in her bed. We were both in that half-asleep, half-awake state. I was flat on my back, with her against my side. She snorted and rolled onto me. Her hand rubbed my chest and she mumbled Halstead's name."

"Wait! I thought you said she was irrelevant."

"I lied." I poured beer into my glass from the fresh bottle. "You want more pretzels?"

"No," I said, "If you do, I'll buy."

He jiggled the basket. "Naw."

"Well, I didn't mind that she called me Halstead. She was asleep. Hell, maybe I would have liked it if she called me that when she was awake. In fact, I remember fantasizing right then and there about her calling me Eric while we made love."

"Is that on the order of talking dirty?"

"Close. I finally went to see him in his office. We were assigned a paper in his class, but it was one of those things where you respect the teacher so much that you're scared to write something that may sound stupid. I wanted his approval before I started. When we talked, he listened to me with those eyes that say 'You're okay.' I told him that I wanted to write a comparison of styles between Kafka and Borges. There had been thousands of papers written on just that thing—even then—but he made me feel as if I had struck a new and exciting idea. He gave me a stronger sense of what I should do and where to go for resources. If I was impressed by him before, I shudder to think what I felt after speaking with him. I was amazed at how young he was. He was our age now: thirty-five."

"Your age, you mean."

"He had a funny stain on his coat that day. I don't know what it was exactly, but it looked like food. There he sat, in his light-blue coat, his hair ruffled nicely, and a stain on his sleeve. Just a small one, but as I sat there talking about the paper, the stain seemed to grow. On someone else, it might have struck me as sloppiness, or I would have ignored the whole thing after my initial note. With him, though, the stain proved something. I don't know what, really, but I had the sense of it being proof. A feeling that the stain belonged there. It authenticated his ruffled hair, his comfortable coat, his red eyes, his very personality. That's it: It vindicated my perception of him. Cassandra, for some reason, saw him with blond hair and green eyes. The stain proved that she was wrong; I was right. I bought another sport coat."

Al snickered. "Did you put a stain on the first one?"

"No, but I did hope it would happen. I began wearing the coat to dinner. And I always put my elbows on the table. Never happened, though. I went to various shoe stores to buy a pair just like his. Soon after, I started following him around the hallways more often. I wanted to catch him at all times so that I could see how he behaved. When I spoke with Cassandra in school, I leaned against the wall with one foot up just like Professor Halstead. I talked to other professors about him, hoping to find out all I could. He was single, or at least divorced. No kids. That made me wonder about his sex life. I imagined him taking home a few co-eds a week. It was clear enough that if he'd wanted to, he could have. I'm sure he had the same response from every class he ever taught. I imagined him going to conferences and talking knowledgeably about this and that, and having young graduate students flocking to his side, staring lovingly into his eyes. God, how I envied him. Maybe envy is the wrong word. I admired him and wanted to be like him. That isn't envy is it?"

"Sounds like love."

"He was perfect. He could feel the pulse of an entire class and know when to go quickly with the momentum of class excitement. Just at a point with all of us ready to burst with a new insight, he would pause and smile. All the fragments of the lecture up to that time, and all his leading questions, accumulated and seemed to be faster and faster coming to that final realization. He smiled and very quietly, almost inaudibly, capped the moment with a single line, bringing it all together. The class as a whole would fall back in the seats and breathe in suddenly, loudly, with a combination of humility before the genius of the work, and of pride in the discovery of it. Oh, yes, I wanted to be like that! I would have given anything to be like him."

"Sounds like you were trying."

"Yup! But now, don't laugh ..."

"Wait!" Al reached out as if to grab the waitress's arm as she passed, but stopped as she noticed him. "Want another beer?" he asked me. His body remained slanting toward the woman.

I lifted my bottle to weigh it, and nodded.

"Two more, please," he said. The waitress stepped away, writing quickly on her pad. "Okay, go ahead."

"Great place to break."

"Sorry. Where were you?"

"Don't laugh, but I began to think of him as Cassandra and I made love. Actually, I was seeing another girl now and then, and it was the same with her."

"That's weird," he said flatly, noncommittally.

"It was like fantasizing while you do it, but instead of thinking of another woman, I began to have pictures of him."

"Uh-huh."

"Come on. You know we all have a little of that in us. But that wasn't what was going on. At least I don't think so. It wasn't really an urge to be with him, or an urge to be dominated, if that makes sense. I would make love with Cassandra and just have pictures of him. Mainly of his face. When more, he was always dressed. I wouldn't feel any less excited about Cassandra, or anything, but just have these pictures. It could have been my psyche's way of dealing with the urges, though."

"Did you ever mention this to Cassandra?"

"As a matter of fact ..."

The waitress arrived with our beer and poured the remains of the old bottle into my glass. She took the dead soldier with her. Al stuck a finger into his bottle and popped it twice.

"What did she say?"

"It was funny: instead of thinking just what you did, she hugged me and said that she wanted to be like him, too. She said that she wanted to be able to instill that kind of excitement for literature into a class. Remember, she was an English major. She also said that she had felt too shy about telling me."

"Maybe her desire to be like him was a homosexual urge, too."

I didn't understand.

"Since he isn't female, she would have to be male to be like him. Then her sexual interest would be a homosexual one."

"Twisted though it is, it makes sense."

"Well, it isn't important, anyway, or is it?"

"No," I said. "By the way, those last two were mine."

"She has the tab."

I took another drink. "So, as time went on, I became more obsessed with him. My mannerisms took on more and more of his qualities. I began speaking of literature as if I knew as much as he did. Of course, with me it must have sounded pompous as hell. Cassandra, oddly enough, liked me more and more as I became less and less of myself. No comment, please. One day, I found myself following him down the hallway, out of the building and to his parking space. I was shocked to realize what I had done. Suddenly, I felt ashamed for having invaded his privacy. I walked away as fast as I could. I skipped his next class. I told myself that I couldn't face those eyes after having done that to him. I derided myself for being so childish, for copying his ways and dressing like him. The awful thing is that I spent the entire class hour pacing back and forth in some graffiti-scrawled bathroom on the top floor. I couldn't tell Cassandra what I had done. Instead, when she asked why I had missed the class, I told her I had felt sick. It was true."

"Did he see you?"

"No. It was humiliating enough as it was." I toyed with my beer bottle, ripping the label in half with my thumbnail.

"So, what happened?"

"I felt stupid, a fool for following him. And this made me want to find out even more about him. It started as a way to discover just how much of an ass he would think I was, if he knew. I became obsessed with the idea of finding out everything. I still admired him—even more, I think, because of my embarrassment. Dissonance theory or something. It seemed like a good idea to see his house. I thought that by seeing the kind of home he lived in, I would know more about him. Perfect sense. And it was easy to find his address. It took me much longer to decide whether or not I should go to his house, but the more I thought, the more the affirmative answer became the right one. Moreover, I knew that I had to follow him home secretively. No one must know.

"I decided to go on a Friday night. It would be best since he had a late class. I parked my car on campus—illegally, of course. That afternoon, in his class, I reached out as a girl headed down the steps to him. 'What color hair does Mr. Halstead have?' I asked. She looked at me as if I were crazy. 'No, I'm serious. I want to know.' 'Blond,' she answered, and hurried away from me. I sat back in the chair. It was right that I asked on the day I was to follow him. It was right that she had answered me in that way. Even if she had said 'black,' I would have heard 'blond.' I knew she saw green eyes."

Al looked at me with a puzzled expression.

"The night began very ordinarily. Straight after five, when he left, I followed. He stopped at a restaurant before going home. I waited in the parking lot with a text for his class and a ham sandwich. I felt tempted to enter and use the restroom just to see what he had ordered, but decided against it. Twice, I nearly reached my limit for patience. The first time, an ice cream truck stopped down the street. Children poured from buildings and alleyways. The second time—an hour and a half later—he came out. From there, he stopped at a grocery."

"You're making this up, right?"

"I waited for him in the parking lot beside the store. He came out with two bags, which he struggled with before putting them into the car. He stopped one last time to fill his tank with gas. So, by the time he pulled into the driveway, it was already dark. Eight or eight-thirty. From where I waited, I could see him open his door. He went back to the car for the groceries, and entered the house. I remember thinking it odd that he didn't turn lights on. The house remained dark. Finally, however, I saw a light go on in what I assumed to be the kitchen. I got out and sneaked around to the side. Luckily, he had bushes surrounding the house. The evergreens climbed up to each window. I looked into the kitchen just as he turned the lights off.

The change startled me, and I forgot to duck down. When I did crouch, I was scared that he had seen me through the window. I sat, frozen to the ground. I waited, but nothing happened. Suddenly, a yellow light shone down from the upstairs and onto the ground a few feet behind me. The light cascaded alongside a large tree that rose well above the rooftop.

"As I sat there, feeling frightened at nearly getting caught, I remembered my shame at following him to his car. The same urge to run hit me, but there—after taking the premeditated step of going to his house—the shame made me want to carry the thing out to its completion. I had already degraded myself, and running would not erase that. I had to do exactly what I had come to do: spy on him. It was humiliating. To sneak around his house and spy on him like a common burglar? But you know that we can't feel like fools for long.

"It then irritated me that he had almost seen me. The fact that I would follow him like a dog annoyed me down to my toes. I hated him for that. For embarrassing me. He was at fault for making me search him out. And for what? I saw it then! I saw that he had talked to me only once. I thought he had seen in me a special student—with a true interest in my paper—but it wasn't that way at all! He looked at all his students that way. He didn't know me. He probably didn't even know my name. I was another silly face in the class to him. And there I was, humiliating myself again! It is difficult to explain the hatred I began to feel for him. It was like some ugly vapor filling me up. It was like something terrible, perverse, that Poe would write about, because I started to plot how to kill him."

Al laughed. "You're putting me on!"

"No one had seen me follow him. He was alone. No one would suspect me. How could anyone find out? It was perfect. He was alone! Besides, he deserved it. He had humiliated me. He had humiliated Cassandra by making her dress up for him. And he had never even thought about her! He was the imp of the perverse! He was the sick one. Not me!"

Al laughed too loudly.

"You don't believe me. Don't laugh. I knew I could do anything I wanted to him. And suddenly, I felt the release from my obsession with him. It was like a blast of cool air. I had control, not him. He would no longer be in my head when I slept with Cassandra. She would never more say his name in her sleep. There was no humiliation in my being there. It was justice! It was a sign of my power, my intelligence. I was the one to set it right!

"I hurried up the tree to look into his window. As I climbed, the branches tore my pants. I swore at him! He had no longer merely humiliated me and Cassandra, but had now ripped my clothes. It was an act of stripping. He was doing it on purpose!"

"That's crazy!"

"Oh, I remembered Poe as I ascended the tree: 'Every succeeding wave of thought overwhelmed me with terror, for, alas! I well, too well, understood that to think, in my situation, was to be lost.' I would kill him. It didn't matter that it was irrational. It didn't matter that I didn't have a weapon. No! I would strangle the son of a bitch! Smash through the window and choke the fucker!"

"Are you crazy?"

"Now you believe me! Now you see! It's true! I climbed. I climbed until I could see everything through his window. His light poured out, but stopped inches from my fingers. He couldn't see me even if he pressed his face against the glass. And I could see everything of him. He would not escape. I could take whatever time I needed. Oh, it was perfect! Perfect! He moved from the room, leaving the door open. I saw him walk down the hallway and into the bathroom. The door closed.

"His room was narrow and not well-lighted. There was only the one window. On the far wall, a large mirror reflected the inside of the wall nearest me. I could see his bed through it, his nightstand and lamp. It was perfect.

"Halstead returned, wearing a bathrobe. He carried a small book under one arm. I watched as he disrobed and slipped into bed. It was a curious feeling to see him naked. He looked too skinny in the light. His skin was too pale and hairless. I had expected him to be virile and healthy, not emaciated. He reached to turn something on the clock radio by his bed. He seemed calm through the mirror as he adjusted himself in bed. He propped up two pillows to read, his hair fluffing up into a cone over the pillows. He lifted his knees, making a tent over his middle. One hand slipped comfortably beneath the sheet while the other hand held the book against a knee.

"The hatred drained from me as I watched that simple scene. Somehow, I could have wished for something more exciting, but I watched. Maybe it was seeing him naked that drained me. I don't know. I watched him. I don't know how long I watched, either, before noticing that his face had changed. His breathing came faster as he squirmed in bed. I saw the sheets moving up and down. He no longer read the book, but just squirmed in the bed. When I suddenly understood what he was doing, I felt horribly embarrassed. Then I was shocked, like looking terrified down a deep abyss. This was the same man I had admired, then hated! Surprisingly, the urge to laugh never hit me. Well, maybe not surprisingly. Instead, his face appeared so suddenly and vividly in the mirror that I froze. He had stopped as if he had heard me outside. I held my breath. He couldn't see me, but his face seemed so vivid in the mirror that I doubted it. Neither one of us moved. His eyes were like two cold pieces of green jade through the glass. After a lifetime, he carefully placed the book down on his nightstand.

"I waited there, breathlessly, as if we two were just waiting to see what the other would do. It must have been half an hour before I slowly climbed down the branches. I'll never forget those eyes staring at me like the eyes of a frightened child."

"Wow!" Al said. "You killed him. And better than a murder."

"No," I said, "you don't understand. I was liberated when I came down from the tree, but so was he."

"What?"

"I freed him from that role. I freed him from that throne I'd created."

"By making him perverse?"

"I made him human, not perverse. You don't see, do you? Afterwards, I respected him more than ever. We were both set free. I took more classes from him, and learned even more. He became the best teacher I ever had, *because* he had become human. Before, it had been impossible to say that I loved him. Then I could. Like I love you. He was human. Afterward, every time he talked about literature, I knew that he felt it, that literature was a genuine force in his life—in our lives! It wasn't just something to study or to be amazed by explications, or all its pretty, pretty metaphors, but because it spoke clearly to what was real and human. And real and human covers a whole lotta territory, Bub."

Al looked doubtful.

Don't you see?"

"No."

"I made him one of us. He became one of us. Just a normal schmuck who happens to know something about something. He could be here now, drinking beer and jawing, or popping bottles the way I wish I could. He could be you."

"Or you, Naranjo," Al said.

"Yes! Exactly: He could be me!"